The Mystery in the Mausoleum

By Stephen Rocco

"The Mystery in the Mausoleum," by Stephen Rocco. ISBN 978-1-63868-110-6 (softcover).

Published 2023 by Virtualbookworm.com Publishing Inc., P.O. Box 9949, College Station, TX, 77842, US.

Table of Contents

Prologue

THE STATELY WIDOW ENTERED the Ridgewood building in a white mink coat that collapsed around her ankles, and protected her from the brusque wintry chill, but not her uneasiness for today's mission. "Ma, you're doing the right thing," uttered the equally chic daughter. Her smart hairstyle exposed her right earlobe adorned with teardrop diamonds that sparkled in the blustery sunshine.

The somber caretaker of this house for the dead, Tom Ward, welcomed the mother and daughter. "Good morning Mrs. Phillips. Nice to see you again, and I presume this is your daughter, Mrs. Ludwig. I feel like we are old friends, since we have communicated so much about this day." Mrs. Ludwig put out her hand displaying carefully manicured red nails in such a way that she seemed to expect the caretaker to kiss it. Instead he vigorously shook her hand, assuring the daughter that all the plans they had discussed would be implemented.

Mrs. Joan Phillips needed assurances from the caretaker. And he complied saying, "Your husband will be fine. We have arranged for a funeral home in Houston to inter Mr. Phillips in a Mausoleum there. Mrs. Phillips interrupted the caretaker before he could go on, "Has anyone done this before? I was raised that the dead should have a peaceful internment." In a weary tone her daughter Carissa Ludwig responded, "Ma, you know this is the right thing. Dad will be with us in Houston. It only makes sense." Her mother reluctantly nodded, "I know, I know. I just hope your dad is not angry with me." Carissa sighed, "That's why we are here Ma; you wanted to see his casket once more and make sure dad is okay."

Carissa patted her mother's hand, but her dark sunglasses hid the rolling of her eyes. This moment was the end of a long year of pleading and cajoling with her mother. Since her father's death four years ago, her mother had become more and more needy, and wanted Carissa to spend more and more time with her, despite the thousand miles between Ridgewood and Houston. Eventually, it was Carissa's husband, Sebastian Ludwig who persuaded Carissa to have her mother move in with them. Thus, today's event began the relocation of Mr. Phillips' casket from the Ridgewood Mausoleum to the Woodlawn Mausoleum in Houston.

Mrs. Phillips had insisted on making sure it was the right person being moved. Carissa could only thank God that her mother didn't want to actually open the casket. As the men prepared to unscrew the facing marble of her dad's crypt, Carissa could not help think that her husband was right. Her father was not really here – death simply was the end of life. No need for tears or expensive funerals as the body had no more meaning. Sebastian Ludwig, an heir to the Ludwig Fiduciary Fund, one of the largest mutual funds in the world, liked to brag that he buried his dad in a pine box. Thus, Carissa believed this whole relocation was a charade simply to get her mom to relocate.

Not that Carissa would do much of the caring. Sebastian had insisted on a 3,000 sq. ft. private wing added to their Houston mansion, with a full-time caretaker for his mother-in-law. With frequent European skiing vacations and Caribbean yachting trips, the Ludwig's were away from their Houston mansion more than in it. "Well, at least the Houston high society gossipers could not allege I did not do right for my mother," Carissa told herself.

Mother and daughter watched as the last screws were removed. They watched as the men carefully unhinged the Italian marble with the template Franklin M. Phillips, 1935-2006. The gasps of the attendants drew mother and daughter to the crypt opening. Carissa's screams were not heard by her mother. Joan had fainted as soon as her eyes adjusted to the dark hole that once held her husband. Carissa's screams echoed through the cathedral like mausoleum. They seemed to defy her husband's posture that a dead human body had no meaning.

Chapter 1: The Walk

"APACHE, GET MY LEG." A quizzical look came over the black and white Collie/Shepard mix. The just awakened Casey let out a laugh, "I know girl. You would get it if you could lift it." That Casey believed with all his heart. In fact, he trusted his service dog Apache more than he trusted most people. If not for Apache, he might not have survived the loss of his leg. As he consciously blocked out the harmful thoughts he once had, he thought to himself, "I love this dog so much that if I had to choose my missing leg or Apache, I would take Apache."

Chastising himself for leaving his leg across the living room, Casey slid down off the couch. As he butted himself over to his V.A. provided right leg, Casey laughed, "Thank God no one can see my ass cheeks sliding over the rug."

In two minutes, Casey had his right leg attached to his calf, just below his right knee. So smooth was his walk that many did not know he was an amputee. Casey recalled those early days in the VA's amputation rehabilitation program. Then it had taken him nearly an hour to attach the leg. Today attaching his leg was as easy as putting on contact lenses.

"Come on girl, let's go for our walk." This was Casey's favorite part of the day. The constant demons that he carried like a persistent wart were forgotten for a bit. Apache also looked forward to these excursions. She knew that if she got lucky, and the cemetery was empty, she might be able to run free.

On this brisk December day in 2010, Casey told Apache that their daily walk in Ridgewood Cemetery would have to be a quick one. "I got to get to work girl. Red called an early meeting."

Casey's home was literally across the street from the finest piece of land in Ridgewood. Some in the town found it a bit ironic that the best land was reserved for the dead, and not the living. Since it was a memorial park, it had no headstones, only bronze markers that lay flat in the ground. Visitors simply saw postcard green rolling hills surrounded by ancient willow and elm trees that resembled ghoulish living creatures in the twilight. In the center of the cemetery stood a church-like structure, a recent addition to Ridgewood Cemetery. It was the Ridgewood Mausoleum. Cemetery officials said that it was built for those in the community who wanted to be above ground. Opened in the last decade, it housed 155 decedents, but had room for approximately 100 more Ridgewood residents. Some Ridgewood folks laughed that the Mausoleum residents were starving the poor bugs in the ground.

Casey often visited the mausoleum on his walks with Apache. With its vaulted roof, stained glass, and Italian marble corridors, the magnificent building looked like a church. Casey frequently lingered in the serene building, which quieted his angst.

On this morning's walk Casey quickly observed that the cemetery was unusually quiet. "I guess no one's getting planted today, huh Apache?" Casey knew that most funerals occurred in the morning. That was why he preferred to take his walks in the early evening when those mystical trees seemed to be alive. "Red thinks I'm crazy to walk around here," Casey laughed to himself. Chester "Red" Atkins was his boss and chief detective at the Ridgewood Police Department. "But he doesn't understand; no one understands me. My two best friends are with me here." Again, Casey had to consciously remove Quinny and Ziggy out of his mind, or else he would be useless for the day.

Seeing that the cemetery was devoid of the living, Casey unleased Apache, who was quickly sniffing the nearby elm tree. She then excitedly went over the ridge of the cemetery, and disappeared from Casey's view.

"Get this fucking dog out of here!" Casey heard the words before seeing the strange figure lying prone on the ground. Initially angered by the tone, Casey was taken aback by the sight before him. As a reproached Apache retreated to Casey's side, the man waved a metal wire brush in the air. Only seconds earlier the same brush was vigorously scrubbing one of the bronze markers that lay flat on the ground. As the man waved the brush, Casey thought he saw a small gun fall out of the diminutive man's pocket. But the man quickly grabbed the object and put it back.

Not sure what he had seen, Casey's mind was soon distracted by something else. As the man rose from the grave, Casey could not conceal his amazement at the sight. This unusual person's head did not match his body. The body was almost elflike, just over five feet tall. There was a large hump on his back that almost pushed the man's head under his shoulders. The head seemed enormous. It resembled a large acorn with a large crown. Just below the sloping forehead were deep coal-colored eyes. The man had a crooked nose, small mouth, and a long pointed chin. He was certainly not a handsome man Casey thought, but this man had a visage one paid attention to. It was those eyes, black pearls that shown with an intensity Casey had not seen since his service in Iraq. Life or death eyes, that conveyed whatever was occurring in the brain was serious business.

As Apache tugged on Casey's trousers to run free again, or perhaps run from the strange man, Casey became curious. "Is that a loved one of yours?" The small man hesitated for about twenty seconds, his eyes never leaving Casey's before responding, "My son Benjamin – he was only six months old." Casey slowly walked over to the bronze marker, scrubbed so finely it looked like it was placed yesterday. It read: *Benjamin A. Stoop, January 3, 1998 –June 6, 1998.*

Casey said softly, "Your son?" "Yup," said the man, retreating to his knees and burnishing the bronze that needed no burnishing. "My son died of SIDS." He looked up at Casey as if observing his reaction to the news. Then he added, "Yes my baby left me." Ignoring this odd comment, Casey put out his hand as the man finally rose. "My name is Casey Conley. I'm sorry for your loss." The man with the large head remained mute, but briefly touched Casey's hand. "I've seen you here before," he responded. After an awkward silence Casey asked the man's name. "I'm Bert, Bert Stoop."

Finally acknowledging Apache's frantic desire to leave, Casey said, "I have to go to work Bert, but it was nice to meet you." Bert simply grunted as he returned to attend to his son's grave. Casey was about to step away when he heard again from Bert. "My wife couldn't handle it when my son died." Casey turned back to Bert, whose dark eyes moistened. "My wife developed a mental condition and couldn't get out of bed for weeks. One day she simply disappeared."

What struck Casey more than Bert's words was his tone. His tears seemed to be ones of anger, and not sadness or regret. Again, an uncomfortable silence developed between the two as Bert once more went back to his knees. Casey finally said, "I'm sorry Bert. I'm a detective with the Ridgewood Police Department. If I can ever help you with anything, please let me know." Bert just grunted.

As Casey was about to leave he noticed a buzz of activity near the mausoleum below the bluff where they stood. A swirl of police cars and ambulances surrounded the palatial building. Bert remarked, "They might need your help over there."

"I know," said a dispirited Casey.

Chapter 2: The Investigation

One Year Later...

"YES, MR. MAYOR, I know these families want answers. I can imagine how I would feel if my loved one was missing for a year. And yes, I know it's an election year." Chester "Red" Atkins rubbed what was left of his once famous red hair, which was now a burnt orange with bursts of silver.

Casey walked into the decrepit basement of the Ridgewood Police Station and knew immediately what the Mayor was complaining about. It was nearly one year since the Ridgewood Mausoleum had been the site of the town's most infamous crime. Someone had removed nine decedents from the mausoleum, and the crime was no closer to being solved now than the day it had occurred. The bodies still had not been recovered.

"Okay Mr. Mayor, if that's the direction you want to go I'm fine with it. In fact, retirement is looking better and better to me." Casey watched as Red made these comments, not in anger, but more in frustration. Everyone knew Red would never retire without solving this crime, so great was his reputation. Even the frustrated Mayor realized he could never replace a Red Atkins, without risking his own reelection.

Chester "Red" Atkins was a living legend in the town of Ridgewood. A superb quarterback in the town's high school, he rebuffed a Division one football scholarship to enlist in the Marines. He served with distinction in Vietnam, receiving the Bronze Star during two tours of duty. Rumor has it that he was part of the historic battle of Khe Sanh, in which 6,000 Marines successfully defended a base camp near Laos from 30,000 communist invaders. The humble Red would never discuss his war experiences. In fact, his experience in Vietnam was revealed to the townsfolk by an eager student conducting a local Veteran's project.

Red was very supportive of all veterans. When the Chief of Police hesitated in hiring a one-legged Casey, it was Red who intervened and recruited Casey to his detective squad.

Nearly fifty-five, Red had been the Chief of Ridgewood detectives for the past ten years. His rise in the police department was meteoric, and he easily could have been the Department's Chief of Police. Physically, he commanded respect. Nearly six feet tall, he had deep set blue eyes, a crooked Roman nose, (a gift from the football field), and a strong mouth and chin. His fair English skin now took on the ruddy complexion of a November pumpkin. The bald dome of his head matched his visage – any "red" left, intermingled with tightly curled gray around his ears.

Red made an instant impression as a first year patrolman. Off duty, and without his gun, Red found himself in the midst of a bank robbery. With the aid of a retiree's cane, Red successfully chased the armed suspects out of the bank. Red became a hero, and then more citations followed – rescuing Ridgewood skaters in a pond, saving an elderly woman from her burning vehicle, and breaking open a banker's Ponzi conspiracy scheme that saved thousands of Ridgewood citizens from losing their meager savings. And as Chief of Detectives for the past ten years, Red had also identified and shut down an opioid "pill mill" operation involving crooked physicians and pharmacists in the town.

But Red's proudest accomplishments were saved for Ridgewood's students. He enjoyed career days and veterans' day affairs at all of Ridgewood's schools. His identification of the opioid problem originated at one of these appearances, when students told him about those pink pills being sold at the schools. To Red, optimistic young people could solve all of America's ills, and he loved to fuel that malleable optimism.

Red's personal life, however, was filled with heartbreak. Returning from Vietnam, Red married his high school sweetheart, Julia. The young couple partied hard. To Red, who never thought he would survive Vietnam, drinking and partying was a distraction. It also distracted him from memories of close friends, who never returned from the war.

With the birth of his two children, Chester Jr. and Alyssa, born a year apart, his party days ended. Not so for his wife Julia, however. He watched as her drinking escalated to the point that her first drink started when he began his morning shift. Attempts at rehabilitation failed, and Red sought a divorce when his children were six and seven. Reluctantly he filed for full custody when Chester Jr.'s first grade teacher informed Red that his son had missed more school days than he had attended. A protracted and personal custody battle ensued. Many friends and family members were stunned when Julia received custody. She immediately moved to her parents' home fifty miles away, in the town of Oxford.

Red's battles with his former wife left his children as casualties. In their rare visits with their dad, both children blamed him for the divorce, even blaming him for their mother's alcoholism. Eventually Chester Jr. and Alyssa refused to see Red, and he often returned home alone from Oxford, despite having weekend visits. Red was faithful in supporting his children, never missing a child support payment. Now that they were both in college, he paid for that too. Despite this, he had not seen his children for five years, and his twice yearly letters to them were returned unopened.

Red had never remarried, and had not had a drink in thirty years. Occasionally, he dated, but the lingering distaste of his marriage often sabotaged any relationship that grew intense.

Instead, Red plunged himself into his police work, and this was the reason the Mayor would never fire him. Chester "Red" Atkins was revered and respected by all.

After his talk with the Mayor, Red focused his team meeting on the mausoleum mystery. Addressing his team with renewed fervor Red exclaimed, "Team, we are missing something! I've decided to start from scratch, and rework this mausoleum investigation."

Red's words triggered a collective recall of the chaos of those first few days of the investigation. Following the realization that Franklin Phillips' body was missing, all 155 crypts were examined. It was found that seven other men and one woman were also missing. Since all nine decedents had been in their respective crypts at least two years, the detectives immediately inherited a cold crime case.

Family members, cemetery workers, lawyers, and multiple news media sources, even national stations, were present as the crypts were opened. Most of the bereaved were relieved. But the eight other families whose loved ones were missing, suffered like Joan Phillips; their grief compounded by the mystery as to why their loved ones had been removed.

Sensing the same sentiments as his staff, Red said," I hear from these families almost every day." He added ruefully, "Or from their attorneys, who allege we are maliciously negligent." Trying to shield his staff from these accusations, Red had all queries from anyone about the case referred to him. Casey and Kim were happy that at least the media had moved on to the next sensation. This would make their investigation easier.

Red continued, "These poor families deserve to have their loved ones returned." The detectives nodded their heads in unison. On the team besides Casey was Red's senior detective Kim Davis. Kim was a seasoned officer who recently turned fifty, and had been a detective for twenty years. She was astute and street smart. In fact the "pill mill" case was solved largely through her undercover work as a middle aged patient with a slipped disc. The matronly Kim fit the part perfectly, and was given more and more opioids without examination from a crooked doctor. Red knew that behind her thick glasses was a savvy investigator.

"I couldn't agree with you more boss," said Kim. "From the first day I think we all recognized that this was such an unusual crime. The thing I struggle with is the motive: Why would someone do something like this?" Casey, largely silent, nodded his head in assent to Kim's comments.

"Let's look at the evidence again," said Red, as he displayed all the photographs and evidence that overwhelmed their small office. "From day one we have been hampered by a lack of videos in the mausoleum. Casey piped up, "Now they have more cameras than a Hollywood movie set." Kim agreed, "I guess no one ever thought people would rob a mausoleum." Red gave a sad laugh, "I know every mausoleum in the country has them now."

Red refocused the meeting. "Let's look at opportunity and means. Who would have access to the mausoleum, and how would they do this? The way the person or persons did this was pretty sophisticated. They somehow removed the marble from the crypt and opened the caskets and removed the bodies. This took some planning." Casey offered his assessment, "Boss, I believe this took a team of people. They had to remove the body, get it on some type of stretcher, and then put it in a vehicle." Red thought about it, "I'm not sure. It could be one really capable person."

Red turned to Kim, "Kim, you have interviewed many of the people at the cemetery. What do they think?" "Unfortunately Red," said Kim, "they said it's not that difficult to access the crypts containing the bodies. You just need a couple of tools to remove the marble and open a casket. With a simple stretcher one person could roll a decedent to his vehicle."

"I see," said Red. "I've also talked with medical examiners and funeral directors who said the deceased would have been well preserved, given the atmospheric conditions in the mausoleum." Kim responded, "Does that mean the bodies would deteriorate outside the mausoleum?" "Well, that depends," said Red. "They told me in the right dry or cool conditions the embalmed body would remain intact."

"What else do we have here?" Kim asked. "We have no forensic evidence. Whoever did this was very skilled at leaving no fingerprints or DNA evidence." Red sighed, and waved his hands over the evidence. "I just feel we are missing something. Kim and Casey, I want you to re-interview all the personnel again – from the superintendent of the cemetery to the gardener. Look at anyone who had access to the building. They had both the opportunity and the means. Kim, I want you to start with that superintendent Tom Ward. I think he could be more forthcoming – he is only interested in saving his job. Casey, you re-interview that Jim Boyd guy. He is definitely eccentric enough to do something like this. All of his co-workers identified him as the most likely."

Casey sighed, "No problem Red. I really don't think that it was him though. Maybe some of his co-workers have something to hide."

For once Red showed a bit of that Celtic temper, "Well, re-interview all of them then! These loved ones are in pain. This case is getting colder and colder. I can't let that happen. Somewhere there are bodies and we have to find them!"

Chapter 3: Casey, the Mystery Man

CASEY SMOOTHLY SLID into the front seat of his 2005 Honda Accord, which was closing in on 200,000 miles. He nonchalantly used his healthy left leg to work both the gas and the brakes. His leg maneuvers were so natural to Casey, that he felt he had driven this way his whole life. In fact, when he got his license renewed after his rehabilitation, the Registry Officer declined to stamp the license as restricted in any way. The Officer had handed Casey his license and said, "I wish all my students drove like you. And thank you for your service."

Casey heard that comment many times from a number of the residents of Ridgewood. "They probably just have sympathy for me." Casey often thought the comment unsuitable. After all, he joined the service to pay for college, nothing more. Just because most of his dreams were crushed in the process, that's the way it was. "I was damaged before the war, and damaged after," he told himself often. "The real heroes were my best friends Quinny and Ziggy." Casey often had to remove their memories from his mind at work, when he sometimes was incapable of thinking of anything else. But these friends were always with him. He had made sure of that.

On his way to re-interview Jim Boyd at Ridgewood Cemetery, Casey decided to swing by his parents' house. "My father is probably at the "V" already," Casey thought. The "V" referred to the local V.F.W, even though it was only 11 a.m.

Casey was in a somber mood. The meeting with his co-workers regarding the mausoleum case depressed him. Up until a year ago he was the happiest detective in America. He had fulfilled one of his two childhood goals. Casey had wanted to be a police officer from the day Chester Atkins walked into his 6th grade class. Chester seemed like a living Greek god to Casey. Fit and handsome with curly red hair trimmed military style, Chester exuded poise and confidence. As Chester discussed the various roles police officers perform in an average day, the young Casey had a vision. "That's what I want to do someday. Everyone admires him." In fact, for an introverted child, like Casey, this career vision forced him out of his shell.

A lackadaisical student up until that point, content to be alone reading tabloid magazines, Casey recognized he would have to change to fulfill his dreams. He studied harder and slowly cultivated some good friends, but even to this day Casey considered himself his own best friend.

Casey eased his Accord into the driveway of the modest ranch style home of his parents. He hesitated before going in. "I wish this mausoleum case would just go away," he thought. It depressed him and it was the first case in which his investigation ardor had waned. "Maye Red will let me work on something else."

Casey walked in on his mother carrying a large load of laundry. "Hi mom," he said as he attempted to give his mom a kiss she did not want. Instead of greeting him, she complained, "Do you see this piss on your father's sheets? That's all I do around here, clean up his shit!" Casey sighed with his mother's familiar rift on marriage and life. "I should just get out of Ridgewood," she grumbled, "and maybe go to Florida." Casey smirked. Florida has been a frustrated destination for his mom for the past twenty years. A small human dynamo, Patricia Conley was a wispy redhead of fifty-five years. Cleaning her home was her passion, and pissed upon sheets made an erratic personality only more volatile. In contrast, Casey's alcoholic father, Dan, rarely said a word, even when his wife berated him, which was every day. Instead his response to her was the click of the tab as another Budweiser was opened. Most nights Casey watched as his mom picked up the empties around his passed out dad's feet, yelling threats at his silent figure as she cleaned up after him. Patricia often threatened to leave her husband, and make a life for herself in Florida. Growing up Casey never knew if his mother intended to take him with her in these familiar rants.

As a boy Casey didn't have many friends, but the few friends who came into his home called his parents the Costanza's, after the Seinfeld comedy. Married to Dan for thirty-five years, Patricia had seemingly been divorcing him for that long. An attractive red head, always on the go, Patricia was just starting to look her given age. She took pride in her appearance, had cultivated a group of close girlfriends, and had carved out a life that did not include her husband.

In contrast, Dan Conley looked much older than his fifty-five years. The many years of alcohol abuse had left him with classic physical symptoms: his slim rangy body had limp arms and legs, devoid of any muscle, and he had a slight unnatural paunch in his belly where his Budweiser's landed. Dan had a forlorn hangdog face with hair hanging over his ears and a hit or miss wispy mustache. But his greatest physical characteristic was his bright red/purple bulbous nose. It resembled an obscene mushroom in the center of his face that seemingly grew uglier every year.

Dan Conley was also a Vietnam veteran like Chester Atkins. Casey's dad never talked about his service, but Dan's drinking buddies at the "V" teased Casey one night when Dan had passed out. "Your father's ass was stationed out in a naval freighter his whole tour." Casey knew that the teasing of his dad was common.

Patricia finally focused her attention on her son, "How you guys making out with the mausoleum case? Some fucking nuts out there, to do something like that!"

"Not much progress Ma. They might not be nuts, maybe more like sick."

"Whatever," said Patricia. "Anyway, how's dad doing?" asked Casey.

"I should have divorced your father years ago."

Casey tried not to roll his eyes at the refrain. "Why don't you guys sell this house? You both have lived separate lives for years." His mother just stared at him as she asked, "How long do you think your dad would last without me?"

To Casey, his mother's response said everything about this three person family dynamic. It took years for Casey to understand that his mother was the ultimate victim. Her pain for being trapped in a miserable marriage was its own reward for her. It validated that life sucks and change was something to fear. Casey's realization about this sad and difficult woman had come under the clear stars of the Iraqi desert. But the memories of the young Casey trying to understand the parental dynamic remained.

As for his dad, there was not much for Casey to understand. Alcoholism had been part of his family for years. Even as a boy visiting his paternal grandparents, Casey remembers at breakfast, the drink of choice for them was screwdrivers. Casey got eggs with his orange juice, while his grandparents got vodka with theirs.

Casey considered his dad like a silent sibling in the home. Dan rarely answered any of the constant berating of Patricia. "What a loser!" was one of her favorites. Instead, the retired Ridgewood postal worker went to the "V" each day around 11 am, and commiserated with his drinking buddies. The only difference prior to his retirement was then the drinking had begun at 4 pm, when he got out of work. Casey thought, "When I talked to my father he would listen to me, but I never knew what was behind those sad eyes."

Patricia turned a wary eye to Casey as she feverishly ironed her no wrinkle bed sheets, "Don't you think it's time you started dating again? You don't want people talking about you."

"No, Ma, I'm not ready. Anyway, I got Apache."

Patricia looked horrified, "Great, you got a fucking dog for a partner." Casey felt the familiar rush of regret. "Why did I even come by here," he thought.

Casey was about to grab his coat when his mother put down her iron. "I hear that Lily is teaching over in Blackstone. She's still not married I hear." Casey hurried to the door, but his mom stepped in front of him. "Casey, what's wrong with you? You know she was the best thing that ever happened to you. So she hurt you. You could give her a second chance."

Gently sliding by the intense eyes of his mother Casey said, "I have to do an interview."

He walked out listening to the angry words of his mom, "What's wrong with you Casey? In some ways you are just like your father!"

Casey drove to the Ridgewood cemetery with a familiar guilt, rather than anger. "My mother's right. I am weird." He realized deep down that he could only show a bit of himself to the world. He knew that people simply could not be trusted. The only ones he truly trusted were his two brothers in Iraq, and look what happened to them.

As for Lily, she simply validated what he felt – the world is out to screw you. She was the first one he opened his heart and soul to, and look at what she did. "I will never get hurt like that again," he vowed.

Before long Casey found himself in front of the Ridgewood Mausoleum. He always admired the rich contours and design of this building on his long walks with Apache. It also housed the office of the cemetery's superintendent, Tom Ward. As Casey walked into Tom' office, surrounded by the dead, he observed that Tom seemed to have aged ten years in the last year.

"Hi Tom, I'm here to interview Jim Boyd again. Where would I find him?" Tom looked up from his desk, "He's out planting tulips in the Evergreen section. He likes to work by himself. Do you think he may have stolen those bodies?" Casey responded, "I'm not sure Tom. All I can tell you is we are reinvestigating all of the evidence. Red is even bringing in an F.B.I. profiler to help."

Tom showed Casey the mausoleum's new security system as he directed him to Jim Boyd's location. "If a mouse farts around here I have it on camera," boasted Tom, "but unfortunately it's a year too late." Casey silently agreed. "Are you optimistic you will solve this soon Casey?" asked Tom.

"I don't know Tom. Even Red is stymied by this crime. But I can assure you he will not give up."

Tom admitted to Casey, "I am lucky I still have a job here Casey. Those families whose loved ones are missing hate me and everyone at our cemetery. And I get it. They think it was either an inside job, or we should have stopped it. But you guys have interviewed everyone here. I don't think any of our employees did it." Casey nodded in silence.

Casey walked toward the familiar, long stooped figure of Jim Boyd planting a beautiful bed of roses. Casey was not surprised that Jim was working alone. His co-workers at Ridgewood liked Jim, but considered him a bit odd. He was the longest tenured employee at Ridgewood, having worked there for twenty-five years. Now forty-one, he lived with his mother in a house not far from Casey's home, near the cemetery. At the age of sixteen Jim had crossed his yard, and began cutting grass at the cemetery. He never left.

Jim Boyd was string bean thin, tall with winnowy arms and legs, and a long face with teeth so crooked his co-workers called him "Sawtooth." But Jim never reacted when his co-workers used that nickname, and they came to respect his gentle nature. Jim rarely initiated any conversation, but would engage anyone who did. He knew every square inch of the cemetery and could fix any burial-related issue that arose. In fact, his co-workers marveled at Jim's quick action, when, one day while they were lowering a casket, a strap failed, and the casket pinned a worker's leg. Jim jumped into the grave and held up the end of the 300 pound casket freeing the man's leg.

Casey, himself, had a positive view of Jim Boyd when the detective originally interviewed him. In fact, Casey told Red later that he did not believe Jim had taken the bodies. Like all the employees at Ridgewood, Jim's home was inspected for a sign of any of the nine bodies. Casey could almost predict that Jim's small, two bedroom home could not physically contain the bodies.

As Casey approached Jim, he called out, "Hey Jim, doing a fine job." "Thanks," said Jim, "I like planting flowers. They are so beautiful." Casey asked, "How's your hobby going these days?" Jim's dull green, crooked teeth barely shined with his smile, "I got a beautiful angel the other day at Oaklawn Cemetery over in Riverview. I got it here, in my pocket." He showed Casey the image. Casey recalled that Jim's hobby was grave rubbing. He was actually fascinated as Jim described how art was created by rubbing a special charcoal paper carefully over images on gravestones. Sharp, gray cherubs, flowers, and angels appeared like museum works of art. Jim's bedroom was adorned with these beautiful images, collected over many years. Many residents of

Ridgewood suspected that someone with that kind of hobby might want to steal decedents.

Casey had a good image of Jim, even though Jim admitted he routinely lingered in the mausoleum after dark. He said to Casey, "It's so beautiful and peaceful in there Casey. I get a lot of my best rubbings from the marble." Casey had responded, "Well, until this case is over Jim, you best stay out of there." It was the one time Casey hid information about the case from Red. "I just don't think Jim was capable of this," Casey rationalized in his head.

Casey made more small talk with Jim before asking him, "Any ideas who took the bodies, Jim?" Jim looked skyward and in a slow cadence said, "I don't know. But I don't think it was anyone who works here. No, I think it was someone who wanted to take care of those people. I'm not worried about those people." Casey was surprised by Jim's thoughtful answer. For some reason Jim's words triggered thoughts of Casey's old love, Lily.

Chapter 4: Casey's Plan

AS CASEY DROVE AWAY from the cemetery following the interview with Jim, he felt his collar tighten. Suddenly, his face went flush and his heart beat like a jack hammer fighting through cement. When Casey felt pain radiating in his shoulder, he pulled over. "I'm having a damn heart attack," he said to himself. He did not recognize his face in the car mirror. It looked like one of Jim's red tulips, covered in rainwater.

Casey sat on the side of the road gulping air. He waited for the heart pain to confirm his diagnosis. It never came. Instead his collar loosened and his face returned to a resemblance of normalcy. "I think I had a panic attack." This was a first for Casey, but he had seen many such attacks from his comrades in Iraq.

After he felt sufficiently calmed down, Casey called Red, "Red, is it okay if I go home early, my leg might need an adjustment?" "Sure thing," said Red. "By the way how did the interview go with Jim?" "Very well," said Casey. "I don't believe he took those bodies. I think we can rule him out." "Okay," said Red, however, as Red put the phone down he thought, "But I can't rule out anyone yet. I've never seen a crime like this – no one has."

As Casey resumed driving home, he became irritated, and blamed his mother for this anxiety episode. Why did she have to bring up Lily? He had suppressed his image of her so well, he often forgot what he had loved about her. But today, he could not control those thoughts. He thoughts turned from anger – "If I had never met her I would not have landed in Iraq and returned a one-legged cripple" - to obsession – "Everything was perfect until she crippled my dreams."

Today all his childhood memories arose as his tired body could no longer suppress them. . . .

As a child growing up in the Conley home, Casey often felt different from other kids. He didn't understand how popular classmates glided through life with a confidence even the teachers responded to. He could never forget a tease from a classmate, or a perceived slight from an adult. To this day Casey remembered that a teacher called him just an average student. Rather than prove that teacher wrong, Casey told himself, "I'll never be more than average."

His mother often teased her son, "Casey, you're too damn sensitive. If you aren't careful, you will end up like your father." She was referring to Casey's tendency to disappear. Rarely sharing himself with others, Casey decided it was just easier to keep his thoughts and feelings to himself. His self- esteem was damaged for some reason, which left Casey believing if people did know him, they wouldn't like him. Casey was content to play solitary video games, and bury his head in mystery novels.

In the spring of Casey's sophomore year of high school (1998), his life took a life-altering shift. It was the second time Casey laid eyes on Chester Atkins, but now as a young adult. Officer Atkins was participating in a career day event at the school which Casey attended. Casey found himself absorbed in the police officer's words. Again impressed with the array of skills required for police work, Casey especially admired Officer Atkins' passionate view that a police officer's true reward came from helping others. This resonated with Casey, as he now saw his future in more concrete terms. Perhaps aiding and providing safety to others would erase the ugly feelings he felt about himself.

Around the same time, in study hall, Casey found himself seated next to the most popular girl in the sophomore class. Lily Courage was everything that Casey wasn't. She was loud and confident, with a million dollar smile, never hesitating to engage a teacher about the unfairness of a surprise pop up quiz. She was vice president of her class, and had recently broken the school high jump record of 5ft.1 inch. But Lily's first love was soccer. A forward from seemingly her first kick, Lily played on an elite interstate soccer club team. She had also led her Ridgewood High School team with 15 goals for the season.

Casey's face reddened when Lily asked him if he thought the young substitute teacher monitoring the class was pretty. "I guess so," stammered

Casey. Lily smiled and put out her hand, "You're Casey, right? I'm Lily." Stunned by Lily's attention, Casey hesitantly shook her hand.

"Do you play sports, Casey?"

No, not really."

"You should," commented Lily as the study hall ended. "You got the physique for football."

Casey left that study hall dazed, but entranced by Lily. She was tall and lean – nearly 5'10" – with straight, wispy blonde hair. She had classic Irish features with broad, high cheekbones, and strong sunshine freckles profiling a heart-shaped face.

In fact, her good looks complemented Casey's, as later people commented that they looked like brother and sister. Early in that sophomore year Casey had exhibited a growth spurt. Always a slight child in grade school, he grew to almost 6 feet. His features seemed to emerge with his body. Even his mother gave him half-hearted compliment one day. "Thank God you don't look like your father."

Casey noticed that year that his classmates seemed to take him more seriously. The captain of the football team encouraged him to tryout. However, Casey himself found it difficult to look in the mirror. Rather than seeing the green eyes dominating a handsome countenance, he saw a lost soul.

Remarkably, over the last few weeks of that school year and well into the summer, Casey and Lily's relationship blossomed. He started walking her home from school each day. He learned that in some ways Lily and he were alike. Both were only children, and each regretted not having a sibling. Lily's father was also disabled. He was an unfortunate victim of a drunk driving accident and confined to a wheelchair. But unlike Casey's dad, Lily's dad Mike was a strong influence in Lily's life. His daughter Lily, or "Muffin" as he affectionately called her, was very special to him and he attended all of her games, his shouts part of his garrulous nature. Mike and Lily's mom, Sue, took an instant liking to Casey. He later learned that part of the reason was because Casey was not like Lily's first boyfriend. Her ex-boyfriend was the quarterback of the football team. He was self-centered, and broke her heart when he ditched Lily just prior to his senior prom, not even having the decency to tell her he was going with someone else.

Perhaps Lily was drawn to Casey because he was so unlike the loud, cocky quarterback, strutting through the corridors. In fact, Lily teased Casey that he could go a whole day without talking. This is the very point that amazed Casey. How could such an outgoing, beautiful girl be attracted to him? But as the relationship deepened, Casey developed a confidence that perhaps the saying, "opposites attract" might just work here.

By senior year Casey began hatching a plan to mold his life's dreams. "I know what I want now. I want to marry Lily, and become a police officer. My life will be complete if I achieve these two goals." Casey didn't tell Lily about the marriage plans yet, but he knew one thing, he could not let Lily go to college without him.

Lily also had her goals. Since childhood she had wanted to be an early childhood educator. Kindergarten would be her dream job; teaching eager, enthusiastic children who were potty-trained. But Lily's dreams had a giant hurdle to overcome. Her father's disability made for a tight economic household. Lily could not go to college without a scholarship. Her competition in national tournaments had drawn attention from some colleges. These representatives told her to work hard and pay attention to her grades.

And that is what she did. By the fall of her senior year, Lily the team's captain, led her high school division in scoring. Casey took some pride in her success as many of their "dates" were on the soccer field. Casey often played the goalie, trying to bat down Lily's forceful kicks.

And for Casey these times alone with Lily were heaven. Just the two of them alone, where he did not have to share Lily with her many friends. With a semblance of confidence from the relationship, Casey also had come out of his shell. Expending some effort he could engage in small talk whenever they double-dated. His grades also improved, as many nights he studied with Lily, but always at her home. The couple made this decision following the one time Casey relented, after Lily persisted in wanting to study at his house.

Up until then he had kept conversations between Lily and his parents brief. He had cautioned his mom not to swear or belittle his father. "When do I do that?" scoffed Patricia. In fact on Lily and Patricia's first meeting, Casey was slightly pleased when his obviously impressed mom took Lily by the arm and led her into the living room, where they had a private chat. However, Casey never forgot his mom's sarcastic comment when he returned from taking Lily home, "Wow, Casey, Lily is quite a catch. Try not to screw it up!"

As for his dad, Casey made sure that the meeting with Lily took place early in the morning, just before Dan's visit to the "V". Lily had only glowing comments about his parents. "I love your parents, Casey, especially your mom. She is nothing like you said." She laughed, "They are different than mine, but I can tell they love you." Casey just shrugged.

This all changed the one night this young couple was diligently studying for finals in Casey's basement. Suddenly they heard a thud above them followed by shrill curses and threats. "Look at your sorry ass! Casey get up here." The couple rushed upstairs to see Dan lying on the threshold of the front doorway. Apparently his friends at the "V" had propped him up on the door. He fell in when Patricia opened it. Lily then saw the "real" Patricia, as she lashed out with any vulgarity that came to mind. "Fucking Loser" became "Shit for brains," as she realized Dan had soiled himself. If she had any realization that a "guest" was in the home, she did not show it. She shouted to her son, "Casey get his fucking clothes off and let's get him in the tub."

Later, when Dan was in bed, and they thought Patricia had calmed down, Lily and Casey retreated to the basement. But they were unable to study. The echoes of Patricia's further debasement of her husband discouraged that. Casey simply shut his eyes, half expecting Lily to walk out. To his surprise, Lily held his hand and said softly, "Now I understand why you did not want me here. Now I understand you better." Casey could not talk. He just gritted his teeth and cried. Unexpectedly, he angrily removed her hand from his saying, "I don't deserve you." But Lily fired back, "Casey you are a good man." And then she whispered, "I love you Casey Conley, but no more nights studying here." This meant the world to Casey, and he hugged her tightly, and responded, "I love you too." But he would always question whether she said these words out of love or pity.

Their relationship was marred only two times, and both left Casey shaken that he would lose Lily. Casey told Lily that he didn't care to go to the senior prom, and would much rather be alone with her that night. They could stay at the house, eat popcorn, cuddle, and dance together, just the two of them. Lily couldn't believe her ears, "I have only one senior prom Casey, and I'm going, with or without you." Casey quickly acquiesced, but he learned a lesson. Don't reveal everything about his needs. Even though he didn't like sharing Lily with anyone, he should keep those feelings to himself.

Casey's need for inner secrecy was confirmed in another casual conversation with Lily. One day driving home from soccer practice Lily gushed, "I want to have six kids someday, 3 boys and 3 girls, all blondes like us." Without thinking Casey responded, "Really? I would be happy with just you, Lily. I don't know if I even want kids." This must have hit a nerve that Lily was considering a future with Casey. "That's a deal breaker Casey – I want a family." Casey immediately retreated in fear, "Of course I want kids – with you." But Casey didn't want to share Lily, even with their children. While a relaxed Lily smiled, Casey again reinforced the lesson: Don't reveal too much of your thoughts, even to Lily.

It was just after the completion of Lily's fall soccer season, a stellar one in which she was named all-state, that she received the good news. Mt. Ida College, a Division II school about 75 miles away from Ridgewood, offered Lily a full soccer scholarship. Lily immediately accepted, even though her coaches told her that bigger schools would be calling with offers. But Mt. Ida kept her close to her parents, especially her dad, who could attend her college games.

Casey had been worried for some time about what would happen as the end of senior year approached. Outwardly Casey was thrilled for Lily when he heard about the soccer scholarship. Inwardly, he was afraid of losing his true love. He couldn't risk that someone else might take Lily away from him. Lily reassured Casey that they would still remain close. But she offered that Casey himself might want to date other women.

Casey couldn't understand Lily's response, but he didn't say anything to her. Even she could not really understand him. Instead, he researched his options. Like Lily, his parents were in no position to help him. Even if they did, Mt. Ida's tuition for one academic year was almost $45,000 including room and board. A local community college in Ridgewood had a superb criminal justice program for a fifth of that tuition. But that wouldn't solve his need to have Lily nearby.

He looked into military programs that offered tuition assistance. One, the Army National Guard program combined a "citizen-soldier" concept that perfectly fit Casey's needs. For a six year commitment the program would pay up to $30,000 per year for tuition reimbursement. In return Casey had to commit to training one weekend a month as well as a two week training each year.

Intrigued, and without telling Lily, Casey met with the National Guard recruiter. Learning of Casey's desire to be a police officer, the recruiter saw the opening, "Perfect, you can join the military police, which will help you get a law enforcement job." Casey would never forget the words of the recruiter. "It's a piece of cake young man. Many of my soldiers pay for college just like you. They almost look forward to the weekends away, or the summer training. The most you will probably have to do is help with a natural disaster someday."

Excited, Casey applied to the Criminal Justice Program at Mt. Ida College. In February of 2000, he got the news of his acceptance. As he left home that day to sign the commitment, his mother warned him not to rush into this decision. "You see what it did to your father. All I know is the army is going to own your ass." Casey ignored his mother's words.

So Casey signed his commitment to the Army National Guard. Now was the hard part: explaining to Lily the logic of the decision. To Casey his plan made all the sense in the world. Lily and he could marry after college, settle in Ridgewood, and his military training would help him get a police officer's job.

Casey rehearsed all the arguments Lily could offer on this special night. He had chosen Lily's birthday to reveal his plan. Arriving at her home with roses, Casey would not reveal their restaurant destination despite Lily's entreaties. They pulled up to an exclusive lakeside restaurant Lily had always admired. Upon their arrival, Lily planted a kiss on Casey's lips.

As usual Casey enjoyed listening as Lily carried on most of their intimate conversation. She discussed a recent visit to Mt. Ida College to meet her new soccer teammates. Casey commented, "I was also at Mt. Ida recently." "Really," said a surprised Lily, "Why?" It was then that he revealed his whole plan to Lily. He talked so fast, Lily had a hard time processing what he was saying…"It will be perfect Lily. We will both be at the same college. You can get your teaching degree, and I can get my criminal justice degree. We can fulfill all our dreams…. All I ever wanted Lily is your love and to be a police officer. I want you to be my wife Lily; our lives will be perfect."

Lily was initially so stunned, she did not respond. She did have strong feelings for Casey, but she also had to admit that she was looking forward to meeting new people in college. Although she thought she might marry Casey someday, her dreams were a little less focused.

As Lily internalized whatever ambivalence she felt, she could not ignore Casey's handsome face, which now had tears streaming down. He was so passionate about his plans. He kept repeating, "It will be perfect Lily." Responding to his passion, Lily smiled, "It will be nice to have you close Casey. But are you sure of this National Guard thing? What if there is a war?" Casey reassured her, " I'm not considered active military Lily. Those people are called first. The most I might do is to help put out some fires somewhere." Slowly Lily slid her hand over Casey's, thinking that maybe his plan did make sense.

And for the couple's freshman year at Mt. Ida College, things went as Casey had planned. He was able to take out academic loans for the balance of the tuition. He was happy to see Lily every day, even though it meant spending more time with soccer than he preferred. Casey worked had in his course work, and immersed himself in his criminal law classes. His commitment one weekend a month was a piece of cake.

Following his freshman year, Casey attended his first two week basic combat training with the National Guard. He loved the training and Lily commented that she had never seen his body so ripped.

Life continued to be perfect for Casey and Lily as they began their sophomore year at the college. Days into the 2001-2002 academic year, the couple was lying on the grass enjoying a perfect early September day. Casey was telling Lily about his upcoming weekend duty with the Guard, when a student ran by them yelling, "We were just attacked!" Casey and Lily joined the students that had congregated in the student union watching the twin towers descend like a sandcastle on the seashore. Casey immediately knew that his National Guard recruiter had been wrong. His body now belonged to his country and its freedom.

Chapter 5: The FBI Profiler

"COME ON APACHE. We need to have a quick run today. I got an important meeting at the station. No, girl, stay away from the basement." Apache almost appeared confused as rarely did Casey talk so forcefully to her. Apache quickly forgot to rebuke, and patiently wagged her tail as Casey put on her collar.

Casey was almost eye level to Apache as he got out of his wheelchair. His stump felt a bit tender, as he attached his prosthesis. Thinking out loud he said, "I will have to go to the VA hospital and get an adjustment." To Casey, like all amputees this was a common problem.

Upon the disabled Casey's return to Ridgewood in 2005, he lived in a fourth floor walkup with spotty elevator service. Casey had climbed the stairs with his new leg without complaint. But this was not acceptable to the appreciative residents of Ridgewood, caught in the national fervor following the 911 attack on our country.

Subsequently, a lot of land was found near Ridgewood Cemetery and a ranch style, modified three-bedroom home was built specifically for Casey. This was done by a consortium of grateful Ridgewood citizens, with help from the Wounded Warriors program. The house had no stairs, high roll-under countertops and showers, and wheelchair wide doorways. Casey loved the home and had no problem navigating it. He often teased to Red, "They gave me a lot across from the cemetery that no one wanted." The home also had an accessible, no stair basement that had a special feature – a safe room. Since Ridgewood was in an area at risk for tornados, the Veterans' group recommended it in any construction. On humid days Casey frequently retreated to the cool basement of his home.

As Casey and Apache were sprinting through the cemetery, they came upon the area where Bert Stoop regularly tended his son's grave. Many times when Casey saw him, the odd man seemed to be actively talking to the grave in a strange aggressive manner: grunts, sighs and murmurings. Casey made a point of always greeting the man. Sometimes Bert would grunt in response, sometimes he would not even acknowledge Casey.

Today, for some reason, Bert was in a particularly voluble mood. "Oh, great," Casey said to himself, I really can't talk today."

But Bert got right in Casey's face, "Did I tell you my wife left me after Benjamin died?"

"A bit," stammered Casey.

Bert barely let him answer, focusing his intense eyes on Casey, he blurted out, "Yeah, the day my son did not wake up, my wife Abigail would not even let the EMT's remove his body. She lay in bed for weeks, just staring. She couldn't eat or sleep. I did everything to help her – even told her we could have another kid. Nothing worked."

"I see. That's very sad, said Casey. Bert abruptly went back to the grave, as if Casey's compassion bothered him. His angry murmurings continued.

Not sure what to do, Casey uttered, "Bert, I've got to get to work," and he began to walk away.

But Bert turned to Casey and shouted, "There was nothing I could do. She said she had to get away. One day she just disappeared. I never saw her again. I called your station, but they were useless."

A stunned Casey stammered, "How long has she been gone?"

"Fifteen years, and not a peep," replied Bert.

"I'm sorry, maybe I can help."

But Bert just answered, "Don't bother." After a brief silence, Casey left Bert at the grave.

Casey finally arrived at the station, and the first voice he heard was Red's, referring to Casey's excuse for yesterday's absence, "How's the leg feeling Case?"

"I'm good," muttered Casey.

Red and Kim were looking at the photos of the nine missing decedents. Red updated his detectives, "I got a retired FBI profiler coming in as a consultant. I tried to get the FBI's behavioral team to come in, but they did not have jurisdiction. They recommended this person,

Winnifred Alpert, as a private consultant. A month ago I sent her everything about the case. She should be here shortly to give us her analysis. I hear she was their top person." Then Red concluded with a grin, "The Mayor initially balked at her consultant's fee, until I threatened to retire."

Soon the trio was joined by the graceful presence of Winnifred, "Winnie" Alpert. Approximately fifty years of age, the smartly tailored woman had an easy smile and a commanding presence. "Call me Winnie, please."

"I guess you folks retire early in the FBI," said an impressed Red.

"Honestly, I was totally burnt out," responded Winnie. "Interviewing serial killers and pretending you identify with them is not easy. My son will be off to college soon, and I want to enjoy his last high school year. Besides, now I can pick and choose which case to investigate, and you guys really have a doozy here."

Red directly got down to business. "Any feel for what type of suspect we are looking for?

Winnie answered, "The difficulty with this crime is that there is no forensic evidence at all. You don't know when the nine bodies were taken and whoever took them was careful enough not to leave any trace of contact."

Winnie continued, "In my business one of the first things we determine is whether this is an organized or a disorganized crime. Some criminals are sloppy – especially in crimes of passion – and simply move on to the next victim. That is not the case here. This offender was highly organized to the degree that he, she or they knew that there were no cameras to view them. They probably removed the decedents one at a time, given the logistics involved. Obviously, the person or persons are bright and may have worked at the cemetery."

"We have interviewed and re-interviewed all of the cemetery staff," interrupted Red. "We even checked all their homes, from the superintendent to the gardener. They all checked out okay."

"I see," said Winnie. "The culprits were so efficient, that they may even have some police background. Okay, well, the second biggest question about any crime is motive. What I try to do is establish a profile of the criminal; what does the crime tell us about him or her? What is his signature, if you will? For example, we know the rapist is really about power and control. For some, their gratification is from feelings of worthlessness; for others, it is misplaced rage, often originating with their upbringing. I want to know what the crime says about the criminal. What did they say and do to the victim? What were their methods of victimization? And what other criminals do they remind us of?"

Winnie further explained, "The problem here is it is such an unusual crime. We certainly know about the term necrophilia. While it is not a common crime, sex with a decedent is often about safety for people who have been continually rejected. It is a psychologically safe place for such a criminal, giving power to someone with considerable self-loathing."

Winnie continued, "While I am not sure if that is what we have here; why would the perpetrator take both males and females? There are variations of necrophilia which don't necessarily mean sex with the deceased. A "romantic" necrophilia is an example. For some of these people, the fear of death turns into a desire to keep the dead close to them. It helps them feel alive. Others use their love for the decedent as a justification to not let their loved one go. In a sense death is overcome by keeping the dead close. This gives them some control over an event that they otherwise feel helpless to control."

Detective Kim Davis offered, "So it's possible all the victims might be in a warehouse somewhere?" "Yes," said Winnie, "but I think the perpetrator, and I do think it is one person, probably a male, has them all with him. I say this only because this crime has unusual passion that most people do not share. For most people, there is logic in the old adage, "ashes to ashes, dust to dust. They keep the dead close only in their memory, and not in their midst. This person has a special need to keep these specific decedents close. This is the key to solving the case. He is bright, probably college educated, and hides his tremendous guilt and low self-esteem behind a charming veneer."

"Interesting," said an impressed Red, "You have given us good insight into future suspects. Is there anything you could add that might help the investigation?"

Looking at the photographs sprawled all over Red's desk, Winnie thought for a minute. "I think there might be some commonality about the victims here. There were what, 150 bodies in the Mausoleum? Why did he take those nine? You need to think like this criminal. What does he want? What do these victims provide for him? What are his motives?"

Casey had been quiet throughout Winnie's presentation, but in a soft voice said, "Have you ever seen a case like this, Winnie? What could motivate this person?"

"I only had one case that resembled this one Casey. A daughter kept her dead mom in a bed for several months. The daughter served her mom tea each morning, with a lecture. You see Casey, when I interviewed the daughter she said her mom was emotionally and physically abusive to her. Upon her mother's death the roles reversed. The daughter now had control and berated her mom for months. In a sense she was now the parent, and her mother the helpless child."

Winnie further clarified, "As a young girl the abused daughter had no control. But now, the daughter was in full control, and unleashed all her feelings, both conscious and unconscious. Rather than being repulsed by the decaying body of her mom, she was exalted. All of her rage, fury and sadness were unleashed for several months. That's about the only case I can recall Casey. I'll add that the daughter was normally functioning during this period, and had a good recovery after the incident."

"Thank you," said Casey, as he wrote notes to himself.

The three detectives all thanked Winnie for her astute input. She concluded, "I am available at any time to consult with any of you folks. Please keep me apprised if new information develops."

As Winnie exited, Kim turned to Red, "I'm going to re-interview the foreman at the Mausoleum. There was a code pad to allow access to the Mausoleum, but everyone seemed to know it. Anyone in the cemetery who needed to use the restroom in the Mausoleum seemed to know the code."

Red commented, "I wonder why they did not change that code more frequently."

"Boss, got a second?" asked Casey.

"Sure, Case, what's up?"

"Did you ever hear of a missing woman by the name of Abigail Stoop? I ran into this strange guy at the cemetery who said his wife went missing about fifteen years ago."

Red thought for a moment, "Doesn't ring a bell. Let's look at the database." Casey and Red examined their system, but the name did not register.

Casey added, "This guy I see at Ridgewood Cemetery is always at his son's grave. He said his wife was grief-stricken after their son Benjamin died of SIDS, and one day she just disappeared. The man's name is Bert Stoop."

Red murmured, "Bert Stoop, Bet Stoop....that name does ring a bell. Going to the same database,

Red directly recalled the case. "Odd looking guy with a big head?" queried Red.

"That's him," said an intrigued Casey.

Red explained, "I always thought the name Stoop fit this guy. He was one of the suspects in a terrible case about eight years ago. You might have still been in college at the time. Some poor girl, I'll never forget her name…Shoshanna Adair, was blown apart at her home. A nut engineered a bomb hidden in a Christmas package delivered to her home. She opened it and that was it. The girl worked in Daisy's Bar, so there were many suspects. We could never get any traction in the case, as many of the suspects were transients who hung around the bar."

"Do you mind if I take a look at the file on that case?" asked Casey.

"Sure, no problem," said Red, "but don't forget this case." Actually, Red thought that another investigation might be good for Casey. For some reason Casey did not have much passion for the Mausoleum case. "Might have triggered something that happened in Iraq," Red thought to himself. While Casey never discussed the bombing that took his leg, it was common knowledge that several soldiers had died during the same attack. Red returned his attention to the nine photographs on his desk. He studied them as he thought, "What am I missing here?"

Chapter 6: How a Profiler is Made

WINNIFRED "WINNIE" CORMIER grew up in the small Midwestern town of Summit, near Topeka, Kansas. Summit is the type of suburban town with look-alike houses, a picturesque town common, and a familiarity with neighbors. Housewives provide milk and cookies for their children's friends after school, and gossip over white picket fences with their neighbors. Men help shovel their neighbor's driveways, and lie about their weekly golf scores. Sunday religious attendance is mandatory for most families, even if most get restless around the time of the pastor's sermon.

But from a very young age, Winnifred Jordan Cormier knew this was an illusion. For inside some of these pristine houses there was a lot of ugliness. One of her first fully formed memories was of her father berating her mother for some perceived wrong. Her dad's kind eyes became menacing, and his voice harsh. Her mom remained stoic, daring him to vent his anger. Winnie remembered tearfully tugging at her father's legs, wishing him to become the kind father that he normally was.

For Winnie's father was one of the most respected men in the town of Summit. Herman Cormier was the president of a bank. But his duties went far beyond helping many in Summit purchase their homes. His activity in every charitable organization in the town was legendary. Invariably he led every scholarship drive, or effort to rebuild a home destroyed by fire. In fact, so respected was Mr. Cormier by the community, that the residents repeatedly tried to persuade him to run for Mayor, an effort that he repeatedly resisted.

So growing up Winnie felt special. She saw how the community respected and loved her parents. Attending so many events, her handsome and dignified dad was frequently photographed with her equally attractive Mom, Ann. Winnie often wished she resembled her beautiful, blonde mom. But with dark hair, and dark eyes, Winnie mirrored her dad, in both looks and temperament. Winnie was outgoing, and loved meeting new people, unlike her Mom, a rather reserved woman, who preferred transplanting marigolds to accompanying her husband to another public event. Ann was a very private person, and rarely discussed things with her daughter, even when Winnie asked about her mom's childhood. This frustrated the ever curious Winnie. "I wish my mom loved me as much as she loved her flowers," were words that often went through Winnie's mind.

So Winnie concentrated on being a "mother" to her sister Cassie, who was five years younger than Winnie. Winnie felt, even at age eight that she had better maternal instincts than her mother. Cassie would cry about a lost doll or favorite blanket, looking for a response from her mother. Winnie would roll her eyes at her Mom and cuddle Cassie. Her mom would just watch Winnie and Cassie, and then say, "I'll get Cassie something to eat."

But it was Winnie who was the apple of her father's eye. On his good nights he had a special twinkle as he asked Winnie what kind of day she had. Winnie noticed that for some reason he did not seem to have the same tenderness in his eye for Cassie.

This special father-daughter relationship made the bad nights even tougher for Winnie. It usually started with the front door slamming as her father returned from work. Even at the age of eight, Winnie would take Cassie into her bedroom, settle her with her toys, and tell her to stay there. Then Winnie would go back to her parents, to try to prevent the dreaded fight. Winnie could smell the liquor before seeing the distorted face of her father screaming at her mother. The topic of his rage didn't matter. "Do you know how hard I am working?" "Is that all there is for supper?" Her mother's demeanor did not help, as she retorted, "Go ahead, hit me so I can call the cops."

It was at this point Winnie used her special gifts of perception. As Herman approached his wife with a closed fist, Winnie tugged at him.

"Please, dad, read to me. I have a new book." Herman hesitated, and then for some reason his eyes softened, and took his daughter to their "reading" chair. Her parents' bickering continued, but Winnie was able to keep her father content until his eyes cleared. Winnie got so good at gauging her dad's moods, that she often intercepted him as he got out of his car. She would encourage him to have another "daddy-daughter" walk, which served to diminish his anger.

But the worst nights occurred when her community esteemed parents returned from some social event. After the babysitter went home, young Winnie had to serve as a mediator between her inebriated parents. Each would try to physically attack the other, as Winnie would pull her mom and escort her to bed, and then run to her dad and practically push him into his reading chair. In between these actions, Winnie had to comfort her four year old sister, who was terrified that her parents would kill each other. On one of these terrible nights, Winnie heard for the first time the term "bastard" used in reference to Cassie. Winnie made out their accusations. Her father was yelling, "You fucked a neighbor!" And her no longer stoic mother was yelling back, "He was better than you."

It was these moments that ultimately determined Winnie's career. Winnie hated to see her parents fighting. She knew that she should not be privy to her parents' drunken conversations. But, somehow being in the middle of it all made her feel special – like an adult. She had taken charge. She could manage the adults. She had intuitive skills about people, even inebriated ones, that could help manage conflicts. A few times she even called the police on her own. These efforts were futile, however. The police, immediately recognizing her father, simply had him take a ride to "cool off." No arrests were ever made, even though her mom attacked her dad with a knife on one occasion.

Winnie's adolescence found her more and more successfully managing her family's violence. She grew to resent that role, however. She also became increasingly aware of a family dynamic that blamed all of its problems on Cassie. Both parents were critical of her, and over time Cassie lived up to their sorry expectations. By the time Winnie was a senior, Cassie had become overweight, socialized with troubled friends, and smoked pot nearly every day.

So Winnie did something that defined her as an adult. Concerned that Cassie's situation would worsen when she went away to college, Winnie confronted her parents alone. She addressed the alcoholism and violence in the home – something that was never done in the light of the next day. Naturally, her parents denied the seriousness of the situation.

Undaunted, Winnie revealed the secrets she had learned from the drunken mouths of her parents. "Why is Cassie treated differently than me?" "What neighbor are you talking about? "What are you hiding from us?"

Chastised by his prized daughter, her dad revealed the truth. She was told that Cassie was her half-sister. Cassie's dad was a former neighbor, who Winnie vaguely remembered. The neighbor moved away with his family intact, on the condition that he have no contact with Cassie.

"I agreed only because of my standing in the community." Her mom simply cried for the first time.

Their secret revealed, Herman and Ann agreed to participate in counseling with Winnie and Cassie. While it did not save her parents' marriage, counseling did help Cassie. Both parents acknowledged their feelings, and Cassie went to live with her mom, who benefitted from more therapy. Cassie attended a new high school, where she made healthier relationships. Winnie even encouraged Cassie to reach out to her biological dad, and develop a relationship, which she eventually did. As an adult, Winnie took great pride in her sister Cassie, who became a successful trial attorney.

Winnie's ability to listen, and not judge drew folks to her throughout her college years. From her sorority sisters, her male friends, to even her professors, they were all drawn into Winnie's calm, but savvy orbit. If someone asked her what to do, she would help that person simulate his own choices. She would ask questions such as, "What will happen if you continue this type of behavior?" Winnie realized that people have to chew internally on new behavior before making changes.

A psychology major, Winnie decided to get her doctorate in forensic psychology. She was attracted to testing scientific principles to the study of behavior. Her doctoral thesis centered on the organic relationship between child head injuries and serial killers. Upon graduation she was accepted into the FBI's Criminal Profile Unit.

For all of her apparent competency, Winnie was a mess inside when it came to relationships. Although she dated frequently, she was instantly turned off if someone drank alcohol. The smell of hard liquor straightaway brought Winnie to her home life. She was again a young girl inhaling her parents' intoxication as she put each one to bed. What she had never told anyone was after her parents' exhaustive drunken battles, they had sex. Apparently after the anger drained out of them, in their exhaustion they showed each other love. Winnie heard all the sounds of the lovemaking.

So alcohol and sex became intertwined to Winnie at a complex level. Her own therapist helped sort this out, and as an adult Winnie might even have a drink every so often. But with men, Winnie always thought one drink would lead to much more.

Winnie had a series of short term boyfriends, until she met a fellow agent in the FBI Academy named Henry Mueller. A Mormon, Henry did not drink, which comforted Winnie. He also had a strong personality, which also comforted a woman who had served in that role. Dating for two years, the couple married in 1985. Their only child, a boy named Owen, was born in 1990.

As Winnie and Herman's careers progressed in the Bureau, their relationship grew cold. The comfort Winnie liked from the strong will of Henry soon seemed to strangle her. He wanted her to be home most nights, and discouraged even the occasional get together with her college friends. Ironically, it was liquor that eventually ended their marriage. A confirmed abstainer as a Mormon, Henry did not allow alcohol in their home, and disapproved of Winnie drinking at all. For a long time this did not matter to Winnie. But as the years went on, Winnie started to change. One evening, on the rare occasion they dined out with friends, the other couple ordered drinks. In defiance of Henry's glare at her, Winnie ordered a vodka and tonic. Later that night a huge fight erupted in the home. Fourteen year old Owen awoke and became involved in the argument. Owen's tears renewed all of Winnie's terrible memories. She had seen the ugliness in Henry's face, as she had seen it in her father. That night Winnie realized the marriage was over.

Winnie and Henry entered marital therapy, but in Winnie's mind it was help in divorce counseling. The persistent Henry tried to save his marriage, but failed. The couple secured an amicable divorce, and shared custody of Owen throughout his high school years.

In 2008, the forty-eight year old Winnie retired after a twenty-five year career in the FBI. She received numerous citations from their Behavioral Sciences Unit. Her ability to profile characteristics of a serial killer was invariably spot-on, and she received many accolades when the killers were found.

Winnie now had new goals. One, was to spend time with her son Owen before he headed off to college. Two, was to work as an independent consultant as a criminal profiler, away from the bureaucratic limitations of the FBI. It was at this time that Winnie got the call from Red Atkins, Chief of Detectives in the town of Ridgewood.

Chapter 7: Shoshanna Adair's Murder

CASEY LOOKED DOWN at his abbreviated right leg. It didn't bother him to look at it now as it once did. He recalled the amputee technician telling him one day he would be glad the limb was below the knee, or what is known as trans-tibia amputation. He now knew how right that technician was. Casey's mobility was so good that those who did not know him couldn't tell he was an amputee. His gait was that smooth. And for Casey, except for occasional adjustments to his prosthetic – he called them "tune-ups" – he rarely was without his artificial leg, from the moment he woke up until bedtime.

But today he relaxed on his sofa, leg exposed, with the Adair file on his lap. Beef stew was simmering in his second favorite room – the kitchen. Since he was never going to get married, Casey told himself he had better learn to cook. So rarely a night went by when Casey did not prepare a home cooked meal. Veal Marsala and Beef Wellington were two of his specialties.

Casey ignored Apache's pleas to run at Ridgewood Cemetery, "Not tonight girl. I got some work here." Casey soon became engrossed in the murder of this poor young girl.

Several years ago, Shoshanna Adair was all of twenty-five and a bartender at a rough bar well known to police in Ridgewood. Known as Daisy's, the bar was so notorious for drug dealing that the police shut it down numerous times, until it was finally shut down for good. A medical building stands today on the land that once housed Daisy's Bar.

Casey could not believe the details of the crime. Close to Christmas in 1995 someone left a Christmas gift on the porch of an apartment that Shoshanna was renting. The gift was wrapped in Christmas paper, and tied with ribbons, and a tag with her name. It had several stamps on it, and she assumed it had been recently delivered. The poor girl, apparently excited to receive such a gift, quickly opened the package. That's when it blew up right there on the porch. Parts of her were found a hundred yards away. Fortunately no one else was in the building, but Casey surmised that this did not matter to the bomber who had placed the gift there for Shoshanna to find. Forensic experts said that the bomb was very sophisticated. While the ingredients for the bomb could be easily acquired, the trigger required knowledge of electronics and chemistry. The bomb blew up when Shoshanna opened the package, which required a tripwire not easy for a lay person to devise.

Casey slowly fingered the photograph of Shoshanna that fell out of the file. It revealed an attractive face with a sad smile and tired eyes; eyes that seemed to accept that life's cards were not often dealt fairly.

A victim portrait of the young lady revealed that Shoshanna came from a chaotic family environment. She and her two younger siblings primarily lived with their mother. An investigation by child protective services into possible sexual abuse of Shoshanna occurred when she was only eight. A second grade teacher of hers made the complaint, based on her student's comments. The matter dropped when Shoshanna's father abruptly left the home. Later Shoshanna told others that her mother blamed her for her parents' separation. The family moved so often that Shoshanna and her siblings attended five different elementary schools in and around Ridgewood.

Unhappy at home, Shoshanna quit school her junior year, and moved in with a boyfriend several years older. Unfortunately, he was abusive to Shoshanna. Eventually, she took out a restraining order against her partner, and moved out. The only good thing that came out of that relationship was her son Jason, who was born when she was nineteen. Shoshanna and her son couch surfed with friends for two years. She hung out with bad friends, and got into bad habits of leaving her son with dubious baby sitters. She experimented with drugs, and soon she was addicted to opiates, cocaine, or whatever drugs her friends had that night. Her lack of attention to Jason came to the notice of his pediatrician who filed a claim of neglect against Shoshanna.

This was the awakening that Shoshanna needed. When Jason was removed from her home, Shoshanna immediately went for drug treatments. She engaged a therapist who helped the young mother realize that she was repeating her own dysfunctional childhood. Shoshanna worked hard at the therapy both to understand her behavior and make changes. Casey read the therapist's report which stated she had never had a client work so hard in therapy. The therapist unequivocally supported the return of Jason to his mother.

But the bureaucratic nature of protective service worked against the young mother. When Jason was initially place in foster care, Shoshanna was denied any contact with her son. Eventually, she was allowed visits each Sunday from 12 to 4 p.m. Shoshanna never missed a visit. This schedule lasted for two years.

At the time of Shoshanna's murder, at the age of twenty-five she had made tremendous changes in her own life. While Ridgewood Social Services was initially not happy with her employment at a bar, they ultimately grew comfortable with it. Her work finally afforded Shoshanna the ability to get her own apartment. She attended AA meetings religiously, and her apartment was spotless. She soon was allowed alternate weekend visits with Jason. She was so successful at her job that at the time of her death, Shoshanna had been promoted to manager of Daisy's. Her life was finally coming together.

Casey then turned his attention to the evidence in the file. He noted that DNA evidence had been collected from a stamp found on the Christmas gift. It was deemed "inconclusive" for identification purposes. Casey told himself, "That's the first thing I'll do. Perhaps there is saliva or fingerprints on the stamp." As the police department's technology guru, Casey realized that DNA profiling had advanced significantly in recent years. "Maybe we can get a hit on the DNA now," he thought.

Casey saw that despite the notoriety of Shoshanna's case, it went cold quickly. There were no witnesses who saw someone place the package on her stoop. Several suspects with checkered pasts who frequented Daisy's Bar were eventually cleared. All had satisfactory alibis or were deemed unable to make such a sophisticated weapon.

Part of the problem was Shoshanna's lifestyle. So focused on reuniting with her son, she rarely dated or socialized with others. She revealed little of her personal life to her addicts in AA. This despite the fact she had many admirers at Daisy's. Many patrons showed interest in Shoshanna, but in a good, natural way she told them she had her guy – her son Jason. In fact, one potential suspect, an electrician, was under close scrutiny, especially given his technical know-how. Again, despite considerable investigation, including the interview of his wife, the lead did not pan out.

Bert Stoop's name was provided by only one person, Tina Crawford, the owner of Daisy's. She said Bert was a frequent presence at the bar. "An odd duck," she called him. "He rarely spoke to anyone except Shoshanna." But there was no other evidence linking him to the bar, nor evidence that Shoshanna was afraid of Bert. All Tina could offer was some vague feeling that Bert could have committed this crime.

As for Bert Stoop, he appeared voluntarily at the police station. Denying any involvement Bert offered, "How would I know how to make a fucking bomb?" He even offered to take a polygraph, but Casey saw that for some reason it was never done.

Casey closed the file, more concerned about the paucity of the evidence. "My best shot is having the DNA retested. In the meantime, I think I'll talk to this Tina Crawford, if she's still around."

Chapter 8: Casey's Investigation

TINA CRAWFORD HAD A MARLBORO cigarette tucked tightly between her teeth in the local bingo hall. She sat just under the no smoking sign in the basement of St. Bridget's Church. Her long, dyed red hair hung down into her face, covering the nicotine wrinkles that masked her former beauty. Her long, chipped red fingernails were at the ready to plop down a marker if her number was called.

Casey had little trouble finding Tina, the former bar owner of Daisy's. Everyone knew her, since she was a daily presence at St. Bridget's. Perched on her special chair with eight bingo cards in front of her, Tina said she would speak to Casey, "After this game."

As soon as someone called out "Bingo", Tina told the girls she would be right back, "After I speak to the handsome detective." Tina and Casey retreated to a pew in the vacant church. Casey observed that Tina had a unique ability to speak clearly with a cigarette fixed tightly between her teeth. "I could never figure out why you guys couldn't solve this crime. That poor girl was blown to bits," commented Tina.

"I know," said Casey, "And that's why I'm here. I want to look at the case. I was in college when this case took place. Can you tell me a bit about Shoshanna?"

"She was a good kid. She worked with me for three years. I had just promoted her to manager when she was killed. You know I never worried about being short on the register when she was working. All she talked about was getting her kid back."

Tina continued, "She was such a good looking girl. All the guys wanted to date her, but she wasn't interested that way. She just wanted to talk about her son - "Jason this, and Jason that." In fact she had a custody hearing set for the following month to get her son back. I thought so much of her I gave her a $2,000 salary advance for her lawyer. They are a bunch of thieves those lawyers – they are the ones you should be investigating! Tina thought for a moment before she said, "But then she was murdered."

Casey nodded, "So tell me why you thought Bert Stoop did it."

"Well, first off, the guy gave me the willy's. The big head and the back thing- I never liked him from the start."

"Did Shoshanna ever complain to you about him?"

"No, but that was Shoshanna. She worked 50 to 60 hours at Daisy's every week, but she kept everything inside. She kinda reminded me of myself."

"So you had nothing else on Bert that made you suspicious?" For the first time Tina dropped her tough demeanor, and her eyes moistened. "Look, she had one close friend at work, Linda Halloran. Casey was surprised, "Linda Halloran?" I didn't even see her name in the file."

"I know," Tina said, exhaling smoke through clenched teeth. "Linda swore me to secrecy. She was terrified of that Stoop guy. She told me she was sure he killed Shoshanna. Linda left me shortly after Shoshanna's funeral, and I never heard from her again."

"Do you have any idea where she is?" asked Casey.

"Last I heard she was bartending in Florida, somewhere near Ft. Lauderdale."

"Ok, anything else you can think of Tina?"

"All I can say is Linda was deathly afraid of this guy. Before she left me she said, "I'm next," then she disappeared.

"Thank you Tina."

"I see you don't have a ring on your finger. How come a good looking guy like you ain't married? Got a girlfriend?"

"I got a good dog," laughed Casey. "One girl in my life is enough."

"Oh, you're one of those, ha... You're too serious kid, you should have some fun. If I ever need help from the Ridgewood Police Department, I'll make sure I ask for you. All they were good for was hassling me when I owned Daisy's. And detective, try to get that asshole, ok?"

"Will do," said Casey.

Over the next several days Casey was able to track down Linda Halloran's number in Hollywood, Florida, a short distance from Ft. Lauderdale. This was done through a process of elimination by age and physical description. He placed a call to the home. A gruff male answered – said yes, that a Linda Halloran lived there, and then grew gruffer when Casey identified himself as a police detective. "Hey Linda, some cop wants to talk to you." A hesitant Linda Halloran picked up the phone. "H H H Hello."

"Hi Linda, I'm sorry to bother you, but did you used to work with Shoshanna Adair?

"Yes, but I can't talk about her. I'm sorry." The phone clicked.

Casey told himself he would have to go to Florida. "Red's not going to like this," he thought.

Chapter 9: Iraq Memories

RED, WITH THE PHONE IN HIS EAR, leaned back in his chair in the bowels of the Ridgewood Police Station. Every couple of years during the Mayoral election, promises of a new police station for Ridgewood's finest were made. Those promises always seemed to end after the election, newly elected politicians abandoning the police in a building built when speakeasies were popular. The detectives shared two large rooms in the basement that had more asbestos than light. Red had his own office, an old desk in the center displaying pictures of his kids, while Casey, Kim Davis and their sole administrative assistant shared a large space with little privacy.

Casey heard Red in his adjacent office talking to one of his Marine buddies. "Looking forward to the reunion Doug. Tell Smitty to bring some money for once." Casey figured the timing might be right to ask for permission to go to Florida. When he heard Red end the call, he yelled to him, "Boss got a second?" "Sure," said Red. "Got a reunion coming up boss?" "Yeah," answered Red. "Our platoon gets together every five years. Two got cancer which I'm sure came from Agent Orange. I swear my hair got redder in Vietnam from that poison."

Sensitive that Casey had never really discussed his experience in Iraq, Red gently broached the subject, "You close to any of the guys you served with?"

"Not really," said Casey, then added, "My two best friends died over there."

Red hesitated before saying anything else to Casey. He knew his detective was a very private person, and this was the first time Casey had mentioned his late comrades. "This revelation may explain why Casey never discussed his war experience," Red thought to himself. He decided to probe carefully with his detective.

"I'm sorry," said Red.

For some reason Casey's habitual secrecy escaped him, probably because Red understood the war experience. "I really didn't want to go into the service, Red. I joined the National Guard only because it was a way to pay for college. I wanted to be a police officer, Red, ever since I saw you speak at my school. I remember my recruiter for the National Guard saying their generous tuition program was "like stealing money from the government."

"Right," said Red, surprised that Casey had never revealed to him how much his high school appearance had influenced the young man. "I was told my ass would never be shipped to Vietnam."

"Everything changed after 911 Red. We were immediately activated as an act of war was declared. But my sergeant was optimistic that we would be the last ones called. When our troops rolled over Hussein's forces in early 2003, Red, I thought we were safe." Casey then rubbed his head as if deciding whether he wanted to continue the conversation.

Then his words gathered a new momentum, "But everything changed in the fall of 2003, as I entered my junior year of college. Our Adjutant General told us the war in Iraq had entered a new phase. The goal was to help Iraq form its own government, and to do so we had to clear out insurgents, like Al Qaeda. To do this we needed boots on the ground, and he meant my boots, Red."

"That's tough Casey. At least I knew what I was signing up for with the Marines. You just wanted to pay for college."

After an awkward silence in which Red was convinced Casey would end this topic, Casey continued. "I was assigned to the 95th military police battalion, third squadron regiment, second cavalry unit in Baghdad. The only thing that helped me was I immediately befriended two Army regulars who were in their second tour. Their names were Albert Quinn and Carmine Zaggarella. But everyone knew them as "Quinny" and "Zaggy". Great guys who were former active Army, who both worked as police officers when 911 happened. Both volunteered to be activated again and go to Iraq."

Casey continued, "For some reason they took a liking to me, Red. They called me "kid" but Zaggy occasionally called me "psycho", since he said all I obsessed over was my old girlfriend and my desire to be a police officer. I guess he thought I was a bit weird." Casey watched for Red to react to this statement, but Red's face was unchanged.

"I learned quickly, Red. Military Police really stands for Multi-Purpose Officer. One day we could be cleaning latrines, and the next clearing IED's from the roads. We were just sitting ducks, living in a makeshift American City in the desert."

Red gently probed Casey, "Did you have any interaction with the enemy Case? I hear they were like ghosts in the desert – mostly killing our men with IED's."

"That's true, Red. "As I said, we were sitting ducks over there." Casey then revealed a story to Red he had never told anyone outside his Army unit. "There was one occasion when we interacted with them. One day our platoon was sent to this small village called Salhya, about two miles from Baghdad. It was nothing more than a few buildings in the middle of the desert, population about 300 people. A village elder had requested a meeting regarding some sort of upcoming election."

"When we got there, Red, we could not find this elder. Our lieutenant, with the help of our translator, interviewed some guy who claimed to be a relative of the village elder. He directed us to an isolated house on the edge of the desert, giving some bullshit explanation that the elder was visiting an ill family member. Quinny, who was now a sergeant, was commanded to take a squad to the home. I was part of that squad, as was Zaggy."

"As we approached the house, we all felt something was not right. Quinny directed some men to the back of the dwelling, while his team approached the frontal perimeter. My job was to scour the area for any unusual activity."

"As the men advanced toward the house, I noticed some movement in a ridge on the edge of the desert. I saw an Iraqi about to launch a rocket at the house. I didn't even have time to yell; I just lowered my M-4 and fired. Thank God I hit the guy first. Zaggy and the boys hit a second guy about to fire a second rocket. We cleared the house, which turned out to be empty."

Red contemplated for a minute, "That's the thing about war Casey, that civilians do not understand. It's nice to say you were fighting for some bullshit slogan like Iraqi Freedom. I can honestly say when I was in Vietnam, America was the last thing on my mind. I was fighting in the jungle for the man or woman beside me. They were putting their life on the line for me, and I was doing the same for them. That's a powerful bond Casey, something few people experience."

Red's words forced Casey to look away. "I loved those guys Red. They were my brothers. I only trusted one other person like that." Casey's voice suddenly trailed off. Something told Red not to discuss anymore war talk with his young detective. Changing the subject he asked, "So, how are you making out with the Shoshanna Adair investigation?"

A relieved Casey talked excitedly, "Red, I think we can solve this thing. There were some skin cells retrieved on the stamps attached to the bomb's package. DNA was inconclusive at the time, but the technology has advanced tremendously in the last ten years. I want to retest the sample." Red agreed, "That's a no-brainer."

"And Red, I got a person in Florida who was never interviewed in the initial investigation. She was the poor girl's co-worker who skipped town after the bombing. A witness told me she was terrified of this guy, Bert Stoop. I tried calling her, but she wouldn't talk. I could almost sense her fear over the phone. I would like to go see her."

Red doodled with a pencil as he processed the request from his young detective. "You know the Mayor doesn't care much about a ten year old case. We got a small department and the mausoleum case is our priority right now." But Red observed an enthusiasm in Casey for this bombing case that he never showed in recovering any missing bodies. "Ok, but make it a quick trip kid."

Casey thanked his boss and went home to pack for his trip to Florida. He almost regretted disclosing so much about himself to Red. "Be careful," he told himself, especially knowing that he had even come close to mentioning Lily during his conversation.

Casey had not revealed one other thing about his friendship with Quinny and Zaggy. He was so open to these two friends, he told them everything about himself. For war had built a trust in the recalcitrant Casey. Each day in one form or another, he told his two mates how perfect his life would be once he got home. He would marry his one and only, Lily, and become a police officer, and she would be waiting there for him every night when he came home. The bachelor from Brooklyn, Zaggy countered, "I'm going to have lots of girlfriends when I get out of this fucking desert – a different one every night."

But Quinny, the California sergeant, did not tease his friend Casey. Quinny had two young children and a wife that he also worshipped. Quinny was like the older brother Casey wished he had. Quinny would just look at Casey and say, "I hope all your dreams come true kid." Then he would turn to Zaggy and tease, "Who would marry you anyway?" Casey often looked on as Quinny interacted with his kids on video. At times Casey was touched, and thought, "Maybe it wouldn't be too bad sharing Lily with kids."

Casey was in Iraq for nearly a year when he received a card from Lily. It was close to Christmas, so Casey retreated alone to his bunk to read the Christmas greeting.

In her most beautiful handwriting Lily wrote,

"*Dearest Casey, this is one of the hardest letters I have ever had to write. Since college graduation will occur this spring, it has forced me to consider my plans very seriously. While I know we are not formerly engaged, we have talked about our future together. I think it is important for you to know that I am uncertain about my future plans. Some days I daydream about teaching overseas for a year or two. What I am trying to say is that I am not ready to settle down in Ridgewood after I graduate. I think I need to acquire some maturation before I marry anyone. I want you to know that I admire your service to our country, and perhaps the thousands of miles between us has changed your views also. I just think it's fair that you know my feelings Casey."*

I am not seeing or dating anyone else, and at some level I still care about you. But we met when we were young Casey, and maybe both of us need more time to experience our passions in life. And yes, that might mean dating other people down the road.

Who knows Casey, maybe fate will bring us together one day. But right now is not the time. Please stay safe, and try not to hate me for this letter. Your friend, always, Lily."

Casey held on tight to the letter as tears streamed down his face and smudged the words he could not believe. He read and reread the letter. "She's just depressed. If I could just hold her she would see how great life could be." He folded up the letter and carried that thought with him for several days. But he decided not to write or call Lily right away. He was in such a fragile state that he did not trust what he would do – yell or beg her to reconsider.

Casey's withdrawal had come to the attention of Zaggy and Quinny. Zaggy predictably responded, "It's her loss kid. With your looks, you will have no problem replacing her." Quinny patiently held his comments until Casey was ready to actually show him Lily's letter. He wanted to try to give Casey something positive to hang onto. Quinny's persistence finally paid off. Casey gave him the letter and Quinny studied her letter, and even took notes in order to understand the words. At last one night Quinny approached Casey in his bunk, the place where Casey had retreated to every night after dinner since he got Lily's letter; the place where Casey could be alone. Loneliness with its silence was a comfortable feeling for Casey, a feeling he had lived with throughout his childhood.

Quinny spoke quietly, "Casey I know you are hurting, and disappointed in Lily. But I see some positives in this letter. It's not a "dear John" letter, which I have seen other soldiers get over here. It's all about her, Casey. She is not ready to commit to marriage, and her pain over the decision is apparent. Wouldn't you rather know now, rather than marrying her and then finding out she is unhappy." Casey remained silent. Quinny continued, "The good news Casey is that she is not in love with someone else. I know that doesn't help your pain. Zaggy and I know how strong your feelings are for her. But sometimes that's not enough. It takes two people to want the same things in a relationship."

After saying his peace, Quinny simply sat beside his friend for a bit. Then he said calmly, "Maybe you should write a letter Casey, letting her know how you feel."

Casey cried, burying his head in Quinny's lap. "You don't understand. No one understands how much I loved her. She was the perfect one for me. Other than you guys, she was the only one I could talk to. I just can't love anyone else like her."

Quinny rubbed his soldier's arms, "You're a good man Casey. Look at how many lives you saved that day in the desert. You are a hero. Someone else will see that one day. Things will get better. You'll see."

Casey appreciated Quinny's words, but he knew they were not true. He repeated the words in Lily's letter over and over in his mind until he knew them by heart. As he recited them his sadness grew to anger. "How could she do this to us? Everything was so perfect." His perfect plans were ruined. His perfect life was ruined. And Lily had done this to them, to him. "I should have known I could not trust her!"

Night after night Casey's feelings hardened. He blamed Lily for disrupting all his plans. He concluded that Lily was not really worthy of his love after all. Several weeks after receiving Lily's letter he received a phone call from America. It was Lily. Casey told Army dispatch that he would not accept the call......

"Make sure you have batteries in this thing," Casey teased the TSA worker as he went through security at the airport. "My fake leg doesn't like X-rays." The bemused TSA agent scanning the artificial leg asked, "Lost it in the war?" "Iraq," said Casey. "Thank you for your service," was the response.

In fact Casey's humor deflected a growing uneasiness as he was about to fly. He had not been on an airplane since coming home from Iraq. That was no accident. He would never forget the searing heat and fetid smell when the transport plane first landed in Iraq. He avoided anything that reminded him of Iraq.

Casey's unsettled mind was helped by the smiling face of the stewardess. Smiling sweetly she asked, "Can I put your bag in the baggage compartment?" "No, thank you," answered Casey, gripping the Shoshanna Adair file. "Can I get you something to drink?" asked the genial stewardess. "Just water please," said Casey. Still smiling, the stewardess responded, "No problem. This is an easy flight. We will be in Florida in just two hours." The astute stewardess sensed Casey's uneasiness. "Maybe you can sleep for a while, sir."

Casey took the stewardess's advice, and as the humming plane leveled off at 30,000 feet, he closed his eyes. His mind involuntarily went to a place he did not like……

Nothing was right about the convoy mission that day, he recalled. Their mission was to move communication equipment from their base in Baghdad to Anaconda, a refueling station forty miles away.

As usual, the military police provided security for the convoy. One soldier served as a gunner, manning a .50 caliber machine gun on the Humvee, while another soldier served as a driver. Normally, Quinny manned the head Humvee, but on this day, perhaps to cheer Casey up, Quinny said, "Casey, why don't you be the gunner on the lead truck." Casey had always hoped to fight the enemy directly, but this was rare. IED's were the real problem. The first Humvee had the best chance for action. But Casey was not optimistic, as convoys safely navigated this ride three times a day without incident.

"Try not to hit any potholes, Smitty," yelled Casey to the driver settling in below him. "Don't worry, you'll be able to sleep up there today," called Smitty from below.

Smitty was the driver in Casey's Humvee, and Quinny was the gunner in the Humvee just behind them, as the forty tanker convoy advanced to Anaconda. Zaggy manned the gunner position in the third tank. The convoy was about halfway to the destination when Casey thought he heard Smitty say, "Oh, shit!" This was the last thing Casey remembered before finding himself with his face buried in the desert sand. Dust filled his eyes and throat and the smell of fuel filled his nostrils.

Later, a fellow soldier who witnessed the bombing told Casey, "You resembled a Thanksgiving turkey with your head in the sand and one of the drumsticks hemorrhaging blood."

As Casey lifted his head, and came to his senses, he heard gushing water. In fact, it was blood streaming out of Casey's missing right leg. Still blinded by dust he heard someone yell, "Don't move!" Suddenly, two explosions reigned more debris on Casey.

The next thing he remembered was feeling a tightening on his leg. Someone had been able to wrap a tourniquet on his leg. He later learned that he had less than 10% of blood remaining when medics got plasma into him.

Days later Casey awoke to a tremendous pain in his right foot. When he looked down he saw no foot, however, only gauze below his thigh. He realized that he was in a hospital bed. Looking up he saw a nurse and his company Lieutenant, Robert Mazzola standing there. "How are you feeling, Casey?" asked the Lieutenant. "What happened?" questioned a troubled Casey. The somber looking Lieutenant replied, "You hit an IED Casey. Smitty did not make it. And I'm sorry to inform you that you lost your right leg in the explosion. We are going to ship you stateside to get the proper care Casey, as soon as we can. I am nominating you for the Iraq Campaign Medal."

Casey looked stunned, "Was anyone else hurt in the attack?" Lieutenant Mazzola took off his hat and rubbed his eyes. "It was a daisy chain bombing, Casey. The bombs got Quinny and Zaggy. They both died as they ran to help you. I'm very sorry."

Casey had seen plenty of these obscene bombs designed by the cowardly insurgents. The bomb that felled Casey was designed only to hurt him. More serious explosives were placed close to it with more serious detonations. These bombs were designed to kill any of Casey's rescuers.

Casey's body collapsed. At that moment Casey would have given his other leg and both his arms to save his friends. "They died trying to save my sorry ass," he thought. Lieutenant Mazzola attempted to pat Casey's arm to comfort him, but Casey pushed him away. "Fuck the Medal!" ....

Casey woke himself as he shouted these words in the airplane. The kindly stewardess gently touched Casey's hand, "Are you okay?" Groggy Casey realized everyone seated around him was eying him warily. "I'm fine folks," said an embarrassed Casey, "Just a bad dream." As he sat back, he felt perspiration oozing on the seat behind him.

The plane finally landed, and Casey quickly walked through the airport, secured his luggage, retrieved his gun, and obtained his economy vehicle. "I'm going directly to Linda's home," he said to himself, propelled by an urgent need to call on her.

Casey approached Linda Halloran's neighborhood with some trepidation. Anyone would see that it was a rough neighborhood, crammed with as many liquor stores as homes. Groups gathered on dilapidated streets, brazenly swapping drug packages with one another. Casey was glad he brought his gun with him.

Casey finally arrived at Linda's small, gray bungalow house. A baby carriage lay on its side. Mounds of wet, curled up mail had amassed on the crumbling brick stairs. Casey took an uneasy walk to the front door. The doorbell had exposed wires and was obviously not functional. Casey knocked on the door. There was no answer, but he heard movement inside. He spoke loudly to identify himself.

"I'm Officer Casey Conley with the Ridgewood Police Department. I'm looking for Linda Halloran." There was more rustling, as if people were scurrying about.

Casey walked to the rear of the house in time to see a man and woman coming out of a back door. Casey vaguely recognized Linda from a photograph of the two girls, which was in Shoshanna's file.

"Linda, I'm not here to arrest you. I just want to talk to you about Shoshanna." Relieved, the man said, "I'm outta here," and he walked off. Linda stood in front of Casey. She was a 100 pound mess, with black and blue arms, and disheveled hair, partially hiding her face. Casey knew she was thirty-five, but she could easily pass for fifty. When she opened her mouth, Casey could see she had at least two missing teeth. "Look," she said, I can't talk until I get a hit." Casey instinctively realized she was a heroin addict.

"Can you give me $30?" Linda asked with her hand extended. Casey shook his head, "No, I'm sorry that would be illegal."

"Look, I'm going to be out of here all day trying to get money any way I can. Give me $30 bucks, and I'll meet you here this afternoon. I'll talk then." Against all his instincts Casey gave her the $30.

To his surprise Linda arrived back two hours later sounding remarkably more relaxed. She lighted a cigarette, then asked, "How did you find me?" "Tina pointed me in the right direction," explained Casey. "Figures," said Linda nodding, "always playing Mother Theresa."

"Look, the only reason I'm so calm right now is I'm high. I was Shoshanna's best friend. We worked together for two years at the bar. I was the only one she really opened up to. All she talked about was her son, Jason. He was so important to her. She was turning her life around. That guy Stoop is evil. He told me something bad would happen to me the same way it happened to Shoshanna."

"Wait," said Casey, "the guy admitted he blew up Shoshanna?"

Regretting her drug induced comment, Linda nervously asked, "Does Stoop know you are here? I'm terrified of that guy. He's wrecked my life as it is."

"No, he has no idea there is even an investigation. I'm hopeful that new technology will link him to the crime."

Taking a deep drag Linda opened up, "Look this guy was real sneaky how he stalked Shoshanna. At first she took pity on that toad, when he talked about his wife and son. Shoshanna had a good heart, and naively listened to him. But soon she started seeing him wherever she went – at the supermarket, the bank, the coffee shop. Once she saw him standing outside the hairdresser. I do remember he came up to me at the bar one time and said that Shoshanna reminded him of his wife. One night she finally had a blowout with him at the bar, and he never came in again."

"After the argument Shoshanna thought that was the end of Stoop. Shoshanna didn't see him again. But just before the bombing she said something strange. Someone had broken into her apartment and the only things taken were her undergarments. 'I know he did it. He knows where I live,' she told me."

Right after the bombing I saw Stoop's car outside the bar. I swear he followed me home. Then I started seeing him wherever I went. Finally, I had enough. Leaving the bank I saw him sitting in the car leering at me. I couldn't take it anymore. I was afraid I would be his next victim. I ran to his rolled up window and yelled, "You killed Shoshanna, you bastard!" He just grinned, and drove away. So he never actually said he killed Shoshanna, but that smirk told me everything. He's evil I tell you."

"So that night I packed my things, left the state, and moved in with my mother. I was so paranoid that I even thought he was following me there. I moved around a lot since then."

Casey asked, "I saw a carriage outside. You got kids?"

"Yes, two kids. They live with my mom. I'm working on getting them back. They are the loves of my life."

Casey told himself this girl needed Shoshanna's determination. "Linda, I have some resources in Ridgewood to help you. I can get you into treatment."

"Are you kidding? I'm never going back there! That guy has wrecked my life. I know he will kill me if he has a chance." Linda tightly gripped Casey's arm, her drug addicted eyes absorbing his, "Promise me you won't let Stoop know you found me or talked to me. Promise me you won't tell anyone what I said."

"I promise," said Casey, making promises he knew he might not be able to keep.

Chapter 10: Casey's Regret

RETURNING FROM FLORIDA in 48 hours, Casey updated Red on the status of his investigation. "After ten years, Red, this girl is still frightened of this guy. I think her addiction is another casualty of the bombing."

"That's too bad," commented Red. "Hopefully we can get her back here to testify, if it's this guy Stoop."

"Boss, I said something to Linda Halloran I possibly should not have. I told her she would not have to be a witness in the case." Red instinctively knew that Casey had no business making such a promise in a homicide case. He admonished Casey, "Our job is to secure justice for these victims. We don't take that mission lightly. Hopefully we will not need this witness's testimony, but I cannot honor that promise Casey." Casey knew he was in the wrong, and just answered, "Yes, boss."

"By the way Casey, we should have the results of that DNA retesting within a month. The State Police are optimistic that the lab will produce more specific genetic coding. Until then, let's focus on the Mausoleum investigation."

Red continued, "The foreman of the cemetery, Al Springer, was arrested on a DUI this weekend. I want you to talk to him. When we did criminal background checks on all the cemetery workers his had some activity. Back about twenty years ago, he had some assault and battery charges after his discharge from the army. He has been clean of late, but something may have prompted this arrest. In addition, Casey, Tom Ward, the superintendent told me that Al showed up recently on a video walking around the Mausoleum after hours. Something is going on with this guy. I still think someone at the cemetery took those bodies. They had the means and opportunity. But we may never find out the malicious motive in this case. Al may be our guy. Why don't you get him to come in here for an interview."

Perhaps it was the last comment about motive that provoked Casey to speak without his usual caution, "Are you sure the motive is malicious? I don't think those bodies are being hurt in any way."

Already upset with his young detective over the witness issue, Red uncharacteristically lost his temper. He slammed his fist on the table as he bellowed, "We don't know that Casey. "Just go talk to that guy Al Springer at the cemetery, and get him in here for an interview!

A chagrinned Casey left to interview Al Springer at the cemetery. He had already interviewed Al earlier in the investigation.

Al was just getting ready to leave work for the day when he saw Casey approaching. He greeted Casey with a look of regret. "Hey Casey, Don't know if you heard, but I guess I'll be doing a lot more walking," said Al, chastising himself for trying to drive home after a Saturday night party. "I was so stupid. It's probably going to cost me $10,000 to get my license back."

"Al, I need to talk to you about the missing bodies. My boss Red thinks you might know more about what happened to them. You have also been seen on video tape after hours in the Mausoleum."

Al paused for a moment as Casey watched perspiration gather on Al's brow. "Look Casey, the truth is that I've been sleeping here in the Mausoleum for the last week since I lost my driver's license. My old lady threw me out, and I had no other way to get back and forth from work. I would never do anything like that. I swear to you, I would never touch one of the bodies here."

Al continued, "Look, I've worked with these guys at the cemetery for years. None of us would do such a thing. We are very respectful of this sacred land. If you ask me, it's that guy Stoop. He's always around here, and he knows how everything works."

Sensing his comments also fit Casey, who walked his dog at the cemetery every day, Al corrected himself. "There are lots of people who walk here every day. They are good people, and even war heroes like yourself, Casey. But Stoop is creepy. All the workers here think it was him. Some people here think that he even had something to do with his wife's disappearance. He's your man."

Casey felt his face redden. He didn't like that war hero talk. "I'm not sure about his wife, Al. It's still an open case. How about you come down to the station in the morning Al, for a formal interview with us?"

"Okay, okay," said Al hesitantly. "Does this mean that I'm a suspect?

"Not at all, Al. We just want to cover all our bases," said Casey, a lie made to ease Al's suspicions.

The next morning Red excitedly waited for Al to arrive for his interview. After hearing of Casey's interview with Al, Red now thought this man was the main suspect. When Al never showed, Red called Tom Ward at the cemetery.

"He didn't show up for work today Red. That's not like him."

In fact, Red learned in the next week that Al had disappeared. He had not returned to work, and his wife had not heard from him. An irritated Red put out a bulletin to law enforcement surrounding Ridgewood. But to Red's dismay, no one saw or heard from Al. "He's our guy," thought a dejected Red.

Two months later, without any word about Al, a frustrated Red asked Casey about Bert Stoop. "Do you think this guy is capable of a crime like this?"

"I'm not sure boss," responded Casey. "I could start talking to him a bit more on my morning walks through the cemetery, if that's okay?"

"Yes," said Red. "Good."

And so over the next month Casey and Apache made an effort to engage Bert at his son's grave. It got so that Bert would immediately stop attending to his son's grave when he spotted the pair. Even Apache did not growl so often when she and Casey were with the odd man. Once or twice Casey even saw a slight smile of recognition on Bert's face.

One day Casey asked, "You know Bert, I never asked you what you do for a living."

"I'm disabled. I was working at Armstrong Company, and a truck loader fell on top of me."

"Was that your job, driving a truck?

"No way! I was a tool and die guy. I made the metal forms which kept all those machines working at Armstrong. Completely self-taught too. I was teaching those college kids how to cut and shape those metals when I got hurt."

"That's pretty impressive, Bert. It takes a lot of skill to make those dies."

"Yeah, that's right. My wife used to tell me the job fit me like a T. I liked working alone. How about you Casey; you got a girlfriend?"

Casey shook his head.

"A bachelor, huh. How did you lose your leg?"

Surprised, Casey was unsure how Bert knew that he was an amputee. "I lost it in Iraq. I was in the army."

"Too bad kid," said Bert, shaking his head. Then he abruptly turned his back to Casey, and went back to tending his son's grave, signaling the end of today's discussion.

A week later the cemetery friends engaged again. "Hi Bert, how are you doing today?" asked Casey.

"Not bad. I've been missing my wife today."

"How long has she been gone, Bert?"

Bert stared into space, "Almost twenty years now. I couldn't stop her from leaving after Benjamin died."

"Any idea what happened to her?"

Bert narrowed his intense eyes on Casey, "She probably died of heartbreak. I know she could never love anyone else."

"I see. And you never remarried?" asked Casey innocently.

Casey was surprised by Bert's response. Standing up, and waving his arms, he yelled so loud that other mourners at a nearby grave stood and stared. "Are you crazy?" he screamed. "I could never love another woman. She was everything I ever wanted. She would never have left me if not for Benjamin."

"You mean if not for Benjamin's death?"

"I guess."

The encounters continued without incident until one day when Casey's comfort with Bert led him to ask a crucial question, that he at once regretted. "Did you know the girl who was killed in the bombing about ten years ago?"

The little man rose up from his son's grave to his full five feet height. With clenched lips, his eyes told Casey that Bert now sized everything up immediately. As Apache growled, Bert said menacingly, "You think I killed that girl!"

"No, my boss was mentioning it one day in the office," Casey stammered. Bert's stare told Casey that he was not believed. This was the last of their cemetery discussions. From that day on when Bert saw Casey and Apache approach, he simply turned his back, and aggressively cleared his son's marker.

Chapter 11: Red's Puzzle

CASEY AND KIM WERE side by side in their claustrophobic office when they heard Red scream. At first Casey thought Red was having a heart attack as he heard the wheels of Red's chair squeal. Instead he ran into their office.

"I got it! I got the connection!" Those nine files of missing decedents that had remained on Red's desk for months finally made sense. "They are all veterans. All those people served in the military. Two were marines, three were navy, and four were Army, including the woman, who was a WAC in WWII."

Kim immediately realized the significance of the finding. "I would assume the perpetrators were military also."

"Right," answered Red. "I called the Superintendent, Tom Ward, at Ridgewood. I want you both to go over there and re-interview anyone who had a military service history. We know Al Springer was a veteran. As soon as he's located, he will go to the top of our list."

Detached, but cautious that Red was watching him, Casey said, "Right away, Red." But his heart was in the Halloran investigation. He was on pins and needles as the Stoop DNA retesting was expected any day now.

Kim and Casey lined up schedules with veteran Ridgewood employees. Even Tom Ward would be re-interviewed. With several hours to kill before his first interview, Casey decided to visit his parents. As he walked into the house his mother was in her typical frenzy of activity. In between washing several loads of clothes, she mopped her sterile floors. With no hello, his mom said, "I'm glad you are here. The V called. Your dad is lying on the floor. They are having a hard time picking him up because they are all drunks down there. Go get him and bring him home. I should have divorced the bum years ago."

Casey knew his mom meant the VFW, which she always sarcastically referred to as the "V". Before he left, Casey had to get something from his old bedroom. When he stepped inside he noticed how pristine it was. The bedspread was tucked carefully in the corners of the bed, and his desk and bureau were dust free. He chuckled to himself thinking his mother should be a maid.

As he sat on the bed for a few minutes, his mind retreated to the time when he returned to America as a veteran amputee...

****

Discharged after three months from his excellent care at a regional amputation center of the Veterans Administration, Casey was still on antidepressants. Every time he looked down at his leg he thought of Quinny and Zaggy. "Why did they do it?" he thought. "I'm worthless. I want to be dead." Thoughts like this filled his head. Several times he picked up the phone to call Quinny's wife or Zaggy's family. He couldn't complete the call. "They have to blame me. They must hate me. Those two had so much to offer the world, unlike me." These beliefs haunted Casey.

After three weeks in the hospital, Casey met his amputee coordinator, a prosthetist named Dean Stoddard. Some said Dean never had a bad day, because he was always upbeat and enthusiastic about life. He was a fit 45 years old, who constantly bragged about his two kids. "They are both going to be doctors someday," he would say with conviction.

Casey heard his whistle before he first met Dean. "How're doing kid?" he asked the patient. Casey was irritated by the smiling face and turned away. "Look, you have every right to be upset," Dean said. "My job is to listen to your goals and to help you achieve them. I have quadruple amputees making plans for college."

Looking down, Casey said, "I don't deserve to live."

"Oh, I got one of these. We call it survivor guilt."

Casey interrupted him, "You don't get it. My two buddies died trying to save my sorry ass. They didn't have to die."

After a brief silence, Dean took a serious tone, "Then live your life in glory to them. Make their sacrifice worth it." At that, Casey simply cried for the first time since the bombing. Dean just held his hand.

Shortly, a bond grew between the two men. Considering his new future, Casey pondered what he might do, since police work was now out of the question. But Dean was not convinced, "Not true kid. I have amputees like you doing police work. Haven't you ever watched the para-Olympics kid? Some of those guys run faster than people with two legs. The Police Academy won't cut you any slack. You have to perform as if you had two legs. But with hard work, you can do it."

On one issue Dean was unable to help his new friend. Concerned that Casey had PTSD as well as other emotional issues, Dean recommended therapy. Casey, however, was adamant he was okay. Therefore, other than per functionary meetings with social workers as part of physical therapy, Casey declined any other help.

Over the next few weeks, Dean designed, redesigned, and tweaked Casey's lower leg prosthesis. "My job is to make this custom made to fit your leg Casey." And that he did. Three months later Casey walked out of the hospital with nary a limp. With the help of Dean and his ambulatory therapists, Casey felt comfortable enough thinking that he would never be a burden on others. To Casey this was very important.

But despite all of Dean's optimism, Casey retreated to the mental comfort of "Don't trust anyone, because you will just get hurt." This included Lily. She had written him several times while he was in the hospital, but he threw away the letters unopened. He only had one dream now – to be a police officer. The other dream she had destroyed. Quinny and Zaggy's death meant that no one existed whom he could trust.

Life at his parents' house after his discharge from the hospital was unbearable. As a child, Casey thought it normal for mothers to emasculate their spouses, and for passive fathers to spend the night on lounge chairs surrounded by beer cans. As he got older he tried to ignore what was going on. But Casey's war experience made it difficult to watch the marital dynamic as an adult. The short two hours from when his dad returned from the "V" until he passed out, was his mother's opportunity to trash her husband.

"I should never have married you. You are good for nothing. Clean your own smelly clothes. Why don't you move to the V!"

Casey realized a silent rage was brewing as he listened to his mother rail against his father. So after a month of living with his parents, Casey moved out. Even his parents were startled when he packed his bags to leave. "You two deserve each other," he called back as he left.

****

Casey's recollections were interrupted by a familiar sarcastic voice, "Are you going to let your dad lie in his piss all day?"

Entering the "V", Casey recoiled at the sight before him. He saw that his father had urinated on himself as he sat alone in a chair. His "friends" were engaged in watching *The Price is Right* on television. Casey was enraged, "Couldn't you fucking guys put a towel on him!" They barely moved from their Budweiser's. The smoking bartender responded, "Does it every day kid."

As Casey lifted his father off the chair, the older man proudly mumbled, "My son is a war hero." Casey ironically smiled, because his silent father said only one thing to him as he departed for Iraq, "Don't get blown up over there." Initially Casey thought it was sarcasm, but he later saw that his father knew the reality of Iraq.

During the ride home his dad said more to him than he had in several months. "I'm sorry I let you down son." Casey was silent. Dan continued, "Those people we killed were just peasants – killed babies."

"You mean in Vietnam? I thought you were mostly out to sea."

"No," answered Dan, "I saw the graves. We did some bad things."

"Did you lose any friends over there?"

"Plenty." A few minutes later Dan was fast asleep, and he never raised the subject again.

"Maybe he's like me," thought Casey, "He keeps his demons inside."

Casey helped his dad into the house, where his mom was standing there waiting. "Let's get these clothes off him." Casey watched his mother clean his dad, as she complained, "I have to do this every fucking day. It's not fair Casey." Dan Conley snored loudly as Casey wordlessly left the house.

Casey's next stop was Ridgewood Cemetery, where he and Kim interviewed Superintendent

Tom Ward. Tom responded to their questions, "Yeah, Red told me about this veteran angle. We do have many veterans coming into this Mausoleum. All of the military branches have honor guards they send when we bury veterans. They play taps in the building. Many of the same military reservists do the ceremonies. That means they are in here a lot. I can get you the list of those honor guards."

Casey left Kim there to wait for the list, and drove back to the station. "Maybe the lab will have those DNA results on the bombing," he thought. That was the only excitement he felt.

Chapter 12: The Trip

AS CASEY EASED HIS ANCIENT HONDA Accord through traffic to return to the station, he appreciated the reliability of his vehicle. It had taken him from the East to the West Coast.

****

Three years ago, with the persistent encouragement of his prosthetist and friend Dean, Casey decided to visit the families of Quinny and Zaggy. He remembered Red's words when he asked his boss for the time off. "I think it will help you Casey. Take as much time as you need."

Part of Casey looked forward to this mission, while part of him feared it. "What if they blame me Dean?" was Casey's first response. As usual, Dean had the right retort, "I think it will help their healing to know the final moments of their loved ones' lives." Thus, with his normal anxiety beside him along with Apache, Casey moved forward.

So Casey's first direction was east to Brooklyn, New York to visit the Zaggarella family. He laughed when he first called the home and heard a broken English response from who he presumed was Zaggy's dad, "Youa want to coma here?" Eventually, the dad understood the message. "Bene, bene. Youa stay with us."

Casey marveled at the tight brownstone homes, so close to one another that only a single person could walk between them. In fact, Casey remembered Zaggy saying that his mother would make pizza on their third floor walk-up, and hand it through the window to the neighbor. Casey warily approached the building admiring the neighborhood full of multi-ethnic children playing soccer in between moving cars. Zaggy had once told him, "Psycho, I live in the best neighborhood in the world. Everyone knows one another. I could go to a Lebanese bakery, get goulash cooked in a Russian Café, and find pupusas as good as those found in El Salvador, all within minutes of my home."

Casey, followed by Apache, walked up the three flights of stairs to the Zaggarella residence. Aromas of all types filled his nostrils. Casey was greeted by Carmine Sr., and his wife Lia, who was all dressed in black. With them was their remaining son, David, a pre-med student at Columbia University. The family greeted Casey warmly, Lia even kissing his hands. Apache was fawned over, and soon was contently feasting on Lia's meatballs. David was the family translator, as Carmine and Lia emigrated from Naples, Italy in their teens, and still struggled with English. "Mio bello bambino," said Carmine with an accent that was a blend of Italian and Brooklynese, as he had picked up words from the bricklayers that he worked with. Carmine's calloused hands and thick arms revealed his profession. In fact, his squat, thick figure resembled a large granite brick. His wife, wearing a black apron over her black dress, constantly ringed her hands. "Siede, siede," she said, as she ushered Casey to the dining room table.

David laughed with Casey, "I hope you brought your appetite. My mother has prepared a feast for you." Casey smiled as he absorbed his environment. The dining room was a shrine to Carmine Jr. A mahogany flag case adorned with citations and ribbons sat in the china cabinet. Pictures of Carmine Jr. from kindergarten to uniformed soldier lined the walls.

Watching Casey take it all in, David spoke, "My parents love this country. But the American dream for them has been cut in half. I represent everything they gave up in Italy to start a new life. And my brother realized this also. My parents sacrificed their whole lives for us. That's why it was so hard when we lost him."

"Mio figlio a hero," said a proud Carmine Sr. David explained to Casey that the military officers who came to the home said he died trying to save a fellow soldier.

Casey did not have the words to respond. Fortunately, the distraction of plate after plate of mouthwatering food arrived, courtesy of Lia's magical hands. Some food Casey recognized, such as manicotti and lasagna, some he did not. "This is delicious," said Casey, tasting something new to him. "What is it?"

"Well, you just had cow intestine," laughed David, referring to the tripe Casey now seemed to choke on. But in the end it tasted great, and Casey ate all of it. Sad eyes lit up as Lia sat by Casey and watched him enjoy her specialties. Expresso with a shot of anisette concluded the banquet.

As the dishes were being cleared, David talked about his brother. "My brother initially did not want to go back to Iraq for a second tour. He could have stayed as a police officer, a job he loved. But when he read about the campaigns for Iraq Freedom in 2003, he decided to reenlist. His feelings of anger had amplified as he always said, 'They attacked my city, and I can't forget that.' We are proud of my brother, but it is a silent war for most Americans. They don't know the sacrifices families like mine have made."

His stomach putting pressure on his tight belt, Casey relaxed a bit. He wanted to share some stories about his friend with this loving family. "We called him Zaggy. He was the funniest guy in our unit. Always telling us about the characters in his neighborhood. Bookies, gamblers, and priests, he would call them."

Zaggy's parents leaned into one another, eager to hear how their son was admired. Casey continued, "He was very popular, and very good to me. Me, Zaggy, and Quinny - we were called the three amigos. That's what everyone said." The parents smiled when they heard Casey's last word. "Amico," said Carmine Sr.

Casey inquired, "Did Zaggy, I mean Carmine have a special girlfriend?"

"Plenty of them," said a smiling David. "He liked wearing that police uniform, and getting attention from the ladies.

Casey chuckled, "He always told me to be a playboy when I got home to Ridgewood."

Lia commented in Italian, "Voglio mio figlio sposare una simpatica ragazza Italiana. David smiled at his mother, "She wanted him to marry a nice Italian girl."

Several hours into the visit, Casey sensed that the family wanted to hear more about Carmine's death. Tears started to well in Casey's eyes as he described what happened. "Your son is a hero. He saved my life. He died trying to save me... I'm so sorry."

Carmine Sr. put his calloused hands on Casey shoulder, "Si, si."

Casey then told them every detail about that terrible day. "It was a routine mission carrying supplies over a road we knew well." For the first time Casey lifted his right pant leg, and showed the family his prosthetic. "This is why your son died. I was bleeding out, and my two friends tried to save my life. They got blown up trying to save me." Casey sobbed, and the Italian American family quickly encircled the amputee. David said through tears, "Thank you. We knew he was a hero. He always put other people before himself."

The remaining night was a blur to Casey. Zaggy's family insisted on Casey spending the night when they discovered he was planning to travel across country to visit the Quinn family in California. He awoke to egg frittata, hot cappuccino, and smiles from Zaggy's parents. Hugs and promises to stay in touch accompanied Casey, who was also given a large bag of eggplant sandwiches from Lia.

With Apache riding shotgun, Casey drove almost non-stop to Chicago. The trip gave him lots of time to think about the past......

With Dean's encouragement, Casey took his first police exam in 2006. He did not even get an interview. He suspected his amputee status was behind that. In 2007, he again took the police exam. Not only did he pass the exam, but he scored a 99%. As he prepared religiously for the physical exam he was at first told he could not compete. Casey later learned that a call from Red Adair prompted a reevaluation of that decision. Casey finished in the top 10% of his class, running a mile in less than ten minutes.

Casey smiled through the changing landscapes as he recalled the reaction of his fellow cadets. They could not believe an amputee could do 300 pound squats. "They easily underestimated my desire to be a cop," Casey said out loud to himself. "The day Red put that badge on my uniform was the happiest day of my life."

Two days later Casey found himself in a cheap hotel surrounded by the vast Arizona desert. He fed Apache, told her he would be right back, and decided to stretch his legs. Bored, Casey trudged over to a local pub across from the hotel. Normally an occasional beer drinker, he ordered a shot of bourbon. It had been a long day of driving, and he was self-absorbed as to why he felt so differently from everyone else. Eventually, all thoughts came back to Lily. Why had she messed up all his plans? And then he shed tears in his third bourbon as he raised a silent toast to Zaggy and Quinny. "Quinny, the perfect soldier, should be home with his kids. Zaggy, the hero, should be home with his family. Instead of me. Instead of the worthless me."

These destructive thoughts were interrupted by three locals about his age. Loud and aggressive, they were spewing vulgarities, even though some families were in the pub. Spiked with bourbon, Casey yelled to the guys, "Why don't you keep it down. There are families in here." The leader of the group, a well-built guy with bleached blond hair, and a rather large tattoo on his forearm, responded, "What do we have here? A hero?" This led to a loud back and forth, and soon Casey found himself outside facing the three drunks. Not taking any chances with the athletic looking six foot Casey, they all attacked him at once. Casey did not have a chance, as blows reigned down while he protected his head.

Just then the leader noticed Casey's prosthesis. "Hey, stop it guys. He only has one leg." They all looked down at Casey. "What happened to your leg?" Silence. Then Casey muttered, "None of your business." As the leader helped Casey up he said, "Soldier?"

Again Casey was silent. He wouldn't give these thugs any sense of satisfaction.

The leader said, "I just got back from Afghanistan. I'm a Marine. How about you?" Still silence from Casey. "I'm Sean, and this is Parker and Max." Turning to his buddies he said, "Get some ice for my friend, and four beers.

Finally Casey murmured, "Casey."

Sean asked again, "How did you lose your leg?"

"I was part of the Iraq Freedom Campaign in 2003. I got hit by an IED outside of Baghdad."

Sean angrily responded, "You gave your leg for some people who have been fighting tribal wars for centuries. Iraq, Afghanistan, it makes no difference. They act like fucking animals. We should never have been there. You probably were crippled by an IED that some kid put on the road."

Thinking of the fresh memories of his friend Zaggy's reenlistment, when he could have been chasing women in Brooklyn, Casey spoke with conviction. "We made a difference over there. Those people needed our help and protection from tyrants like Saddam Hussein."

Sean snapped back, "Oh, I get it. You were fighting for democracy over there. What an idiot. As soon as we leave they go back to being persecuted by another dictator. Never mind the billions and billions in aid and equipment we leave there."

Casey had visions of his friend, the beloved Quinny handing out candy to the kids in every village they entered. He recalled Quinny's words. "I love these kids," Quinny used to say. "They are so innocent, and we will give them a better future." More than once he reaffirmed to Casey, "We are doing good things here, Case. We can't let these people suffer. Besides, if we don't take a stand, this evil will just permeate the whole Middle East. The world is a safer place because of our work Casey."

Casey spoke defiantly with Quinny's words resonating in his head. "The world is a safer place because of our work."

Sean spit out his retort, "The terrorists were not even from Iraq. Wow. You know why we were in Iraq? To protect our oil interests. Yeah, our military has been selling this democracy bullshit for years to our young people – from Korea to Vietnam to the Middle East. They create a theme – stop the spread of Communism, or tyranny – and we fall for it over and over. We were used over there buddy. Get it through your fucking head!"

With Quinny's words in his head, and to his own surprise, Casey said decisively, "I would do it again." The man who volunteered simply to pay for college had an epiphany. Here, in this dusty alley, surrounded by three thugs, Casey realized why his friends made the ultimate sacrifice for him. Only in war, with every nerve stretched taut by survival and self-interest, was one's survival dependent on the soldier beside him or her. This dichotomy explains why American soldiers, for over 200 years, have risked their lives in pursuit of a cause as murky as democracy. God's message – to help our neighbor like ourselves – to function beyond self-interest, is the foundation of soldier kinship. Casey realized he was part of a special military family.

With this revelation, Casey felt a peace unlike any he had ever felt in his life. He fell to his knees, and repeated the words with his arms outstretched as if in prayer, "I would do it again."

With that Sean bellowed to his two friends, "What a fucking idiot. Let's get out of here."

Casey sobbed from exhilaration. He realized this guy, Sean, if he even was a Marine, had missed the lessons of this sacred fellowship. He saw the kind eyes of Quinny smiling at him. He could hear Zaggy affectionately calling him "psycho" with his zany laugh. Casey quietly repeated between sobs, "Thank you, thank you," to his friends.

Unsure of how long he sat in that old alley way, Casey still did not want to leave. He felt at peace here. "I would have done the same for them," was the mantra he repeated over and over again.

At some point Casey stood, dusted himself off, and walked across the street to his seedy hotel. He fell into his bed, and had as deep and contented a sleep as he had in years.

As Casey shaved the next day, he looked deeply into his own eyes. "I wish I could tell somebody, even Red, how I feel," he thought. As if on cue, Lily entered his mind. His good thoughts were interrupted. They quickly turned to bad thoughts about her rejection. And soon he heard the voice of his mom yelling at his dad, "Why don't you go to the "V", and never come home"

An unsettled Casey got into his vehicle, and headed west to California. He turned up the radio to turn down the conflicting voices in his head. Before long, Casey could not conjure up the visions of Quinny and Zaggy, despite his continued attempts. The bad had won again.

Once in California, Casey phoned the Quinn family. Nancy Quinn answered, and immediately invited him over. "Don't wait until tomorrow, Casey. Come over now."

Casey was greeted at the door by Albert Quinn Jr., a ten year old miniature version of his late father. "Hello, sir," said the boy looking straight into Casey's eyes. Soon Casey was embraced by Nancy, and introduced to Nancy's husband Philip Woodson. Casey smiled as he overheard Albert Jr. whispering, "Mom, what happened to his eye?" Casey had a black eye, a remnant from his confrontation the previous night.

"Casey served with your dad in the war," she told her children. "They were very good friends." Albert Jr. and eight year old Olivia politely sat at the kitchen table as Casey discussed his ride cross-country, and his life in Ridgewood. The kids perked up when they heard Casey had an artificial leg. Olivia shyly asked, "Can I see it?"

"Sure," said Casey, as he lifted his pant leg. I just have to oil it once a day."

"Really?" said a surprised Albert Jr.

"No," Casey said laughing.

Soon the children were absorbed with Apache, who loved the attention. After some more kitchen conversation, Albert Jr. asked his step-father, "Dad, can we go outside and play with Apache?"

"Sure," said Philip, who joined Apache, Olivia and Albert Jr. outside.

There was an awkward silence between Nancy and Casey. Finally, Nancy said, "I didn't tell them to call Philip dad. It just happened naturally. The kids were so young when their dad died. They don't have many memories of him." Casey noticed a painting of his friend Quinny in his army uniform in the foyer of the home. That was the only reminder.

Nancy continued, "Albert has been gone six years now."

"I understand," said Casey. "They were just babies when he died."

"Yes. You know I get angry sometimes that Albert chose to go back over there. With kids only three and one, he probably could have gotten a waiver. We had such a good life. He loved his work as a police officer here, and he was around every day." She laughed, "He often changed diapers on his lunch break."

She let out a little smile, "But you know Albert. After 9-11 he felt it was his duty to help our country. He said the victims in New York and Pennsylvania were martyrs, and the evil that attacked us had to be stopped. Sometimes I still get mad at him though, but you know Casey, he was such a decent guy."

Casey felt the urge to speak. "The guys used to call him Saint Quinny. He was the best sergeant in our division Nancy. He never put us in harm's way."

"That's good to hear Casey." Then touching his arm, she asked, "How did you lose your leg?"

Casey was silent for a long time. Perhaps his thoughts over the long drive to California overpowered him. He sobbed, "Quinny died trying to save me. I killed him!"

Nancy shot up, put her arms around Casey, and sobbed with him. Both of them in touch with the loss of a wonderful husband and friend.

Nancy finally spoke, "You did not kill Albert, Casey. You may as well say that I killed him because I did not fight hard enough to convince him to stay home with us. He died being what God inspired him to be, a good man who wanted to help others. You know I probably shouldn't say this, but when I lie in bed at night, with Philip next to me, I sometimes think it's Albert. And a comfort comes over me. I then feel that Albert forgives me for remarrying."

Casey returned the message of comfort, "Knowing Quinny, he would want you to be happy."

Hearing the lively screams coming from outside, the couple gazed out the window at Philip and the children playing with Apache. Casey said, "Philip seems like a great guy."

"He is."

Their tears dried, Nancy invited Casey to stay with them for awhile. He stayed two days with the Quinn –Woodson family. One day, as he played catch with Albert Jr. he tried to enjoy the moment.

But he couldn't. Instead he berated himself; "He should be here, not me."

Finally it was time to go, and Casey smiled and hugged the family before the long ride home. "Time to go home girl," Casey said to a contented Apache. But it would be a long time to be alone with his thoughts. Thoughts he feared to have. "I'd better play some upbeat music, not some sad, honky-tonk stuff."

Casey finally arrived at the station. As he walked into the building, he sighed, and thought to himself, "I wish this Mausoleum investigation would just go away." But as he marched into Red's office, Casey knew that this was not possible.

Chapter 13: It's a Hit, But...

CASEY RETURNED TO FIND a somber Red sitting at his desk. Trying to be upbeat Casey said, "Tom Ward believes we have a lot more suspects with this veterans angle Boss."

Red slowly nodded and said, "The crime lab got a DNA profile from the saliva on the stamps, Casey."

Casey was excited, "Do we have a hit on CODIS?" (CODIS is the national crime database.)

"Unfortunately, there was no match, Casey. Stoop's DNA is not in the system."

A disappointed Casey remarked, "That's okay. I know I can get a sample from the guy Stoop. I see him all the time."

"Good," said a still somber Red. "Casey sit down. I got some bad news. I have a colleague down in the Ft. Lauderdale area. After your visit to Linda Halloran, I asked him to keep an eye on the girl. Casey, she overdosed last night. She's gone."

Casey was stunned. "I can't believe it! Do they know what happened?"

"Obviously Casey, she was a junkie. She probably just got a bad hit." Left unsaid was if Bert Stoop was involved. "They are going to do an autopsy Casey. Maybe they will have some answers then."

"Boss, I 'll work as hard on the Mausoleum case as it takes. But I want to try to get some DNA from Stoop."

"No problem," said Red. Just don't lose sight of the Mausoleum case."

"Sure, Boss. I know Stoop's schedule. It shouldn't be that hard."

That was all Red heard about the DNA sample over the next week. Curious, Red stopped Casey one morning, "How you making out on the DNA sample from Stoop?"

"I'm sure I can get it this week," Casey stammered. "I'll continue my surveillance, Boss. I went through his trash the other night, but nothing there. I'll get it soon."

Another week went by. Another week of interviews and cold leads on the Mausoleum case. A frustrated Red sat at his desk and watched Casey conduct a phone interview with a funeral director. "It's strange," thought Red. "I could have gotten that sample within twenty-four hours."

Hungry to solve something, Red looked up Bert's file on his computer. "He's certainly a weird looking dude," thought Red. "I think I'll do a little surveillance myself today."

Red had been sitting outside Bert's home for two hours sipping cold coffee, when the garage door opened. A man fitting Bert's description backed a black Nissan out of the garage and drove down the street. Red was in slow pursuit. Red observed the little man go into the bank and the post office. Then Red followed the black vehicle to the local Nissan dealership. From his vehicle Red observed that Bert went to the service department and the waiting area. Aware that many of these waiting areas provided refreshments, Red decided to act.

Approximately ten people sat in the comfortable waiting room. Some watched television, others read magazines, and others got free coffee. Red immediately spotted Bert and realized that the reports on this man were true. This was a guy you couldn't forget. His physical stature aside, he had an intensity about him. He moved quickly, almost angrily, to change the television station, without asking anyone else's permission. His eyes seemed to radiate, "Just try to say something."

Red dutifully grabbed a Sports Illustrated, but kept his eyes on Bert. In fact, he could not take his eyes off Bert. Red watched as Bert eyeballed everyone around him, making eye contact with Red. Red acknowledged the gaze with a quick nod of his head. Bert's gaze moved on.

Red then caught a break. Bert jumped up quickly and poured himself a coffee; black, no sugar. Red would never forget. Midway through the coffee, a service technician entered the room. "Mr. Stoop, your car is ready."

"You fix that ping in the engine?" Bert said loudly, in front of the bored patrons.

"Yes, sir."

"It better be fixed."

"No charge, Mr. Stoop. Your car is right outside."

Bert quickly poured the remainder of his coffee out, and threw the cup in the trash.

It felt like hours, not seconds that Red could not move. He had to wait until Bert left and hope no one else threw anything into the trash. Once he was sure Bert was gone, Red hurriedly put on gloves and took out a specimen bag. He almost elbowed a guy walking near the barrel. "Sorry." But he had his sample.

Red promptly contacted his friend at the State Crime lab. "Stu, you got to do me a favor. Can you get a rush on a DNA specimen? It's a cold case swab that we are trying to match."

"No problem, Red. Give me a week, and I'll get it done."

"Thanks, Stu. I owe you one."

"Sure thing, Red."

Red waited the week. He was going to tell Casey, but thought otherwise. Actually, he was a bit concerned about his young detective Casey. Aside from Casey's unusual attitude about the Mausoleum case, Red worried that Casey never discussed his life with anyone. In fact, as nice a man as Casey was, few people really knew much about him. He rarely discussed his family. He made no connections to any of his colleagues. And he hardly ever spoke about what he did when he wasn't working.

As a fellow veteran, Red had once gently tried to press the therapy issue with Casey. He shared with Casey that therapy had helped him deal with all the trauma and loss from his time in Vietnam. It was one of the first times Casey revealed his inner feelings. "I'm fine Red. I don't need any help from some shrink." Casey said it forcefully enough that Red understood this door had been closed.

On another occasion Casey started to tell Red about his relationship with Lily. But then he stopped himself in mid-sentence. "It's no use Red. No one will understand." Red again gently tried to get Casey to open up, "It's okay to talk about your feelings Casey."

Casey overreacted in a strange way. "Don't make me talk about it Red. No one understands." He then rushed out of the room. The issue was never brought up again.

One week later Stu kept his promise to Red. "Red, are you sitting down? We got a hit on that sample. The DNA profile matched the stamp sample. It's Bert Stoop. Odds are one billion to one it's not him." Red whistled, "I'll take those odds. Thanks, Stu."

Red hastily went out to the adjoining office where he found Kim and Casey following up Mausoleum leads. Red anticipated that Casey would be angry with what he was about to hear. "I can't worry about going over his head to get the information we needed," Red said to himself. Displaying a hesitant smile he said, "I got good news on the bombing of that poor girl Shoshanna

Adair. It was Bert Stoop. Casey, you should be proud of yourself. Let's get that bastard in here and not even tell him what it's about. We don't want to rehearse anything. We then will spring the DNA trap, after he makes his statement."

Again, Red expected Casey to ask how the DNA was obtained. But, as his colleague Kim slapped him on the back, Casey was silent. "You should be proud to give this woman justice Casey," said Kim. But Casey was strangely quiet, as if in deep thought. Red later remembered that Casey uttered his next words in almost a whisper, "I think I solved the Mausoleum case."

"What did you say?" asked a stunned Red.

Casey blurted out, "You know how I've been going to Stoop's house to get the DNA? Well last night I saw something."

Red prodded him, "Go on."

In an almost subdued state Casey said, "I went last night to Stoop's house. I squeezed in behind thick bushes, and peered into his basement window. I saw Stoop in his basement with a dead body. It almost looked like a skeleton. It had long, white hair and wore a white dress. Stoop was talking to the body, and combing its hair.

Kim, in amazement said, "He was combing a skeleton's hair?"

"Well, it was not exactly a skeleton. You could see some skin on the arms and face."

Red gushed, "Casey, this is unbelievable news. You didn't see any other bodies there?"

"No."

The investigative team took a few moments to process this news. Red's instinctive skills started to be voiced. "We have two major crimes here. If those other eight bodies are not in Stoop's house, we have to find a way to get him to talk. We got him on the Adair case, but we don't know who this other body is. The good news is that these crimes are linked. The evidence has got to be in his home."

Red continued, "Casey, you know this guy best. What is he like?"

"He's no dummy. If he doesn't want to talk about things, he will close up like a clam."

The detectives spent another two hours formulating a detailed plan. Red called in the State Police to help him in the complex investigation. They had no way of knowing that Bert Stoop had other plans for their inquiry.

Chapter 14: The Interview

BERT WAS IN HIS USUAL SPOT at the cemetery tending to his son's grave. He barely looked up when he saw Casey. The two other people in uniform did get his attention though. "We having a conference here?" Bert asked without looking up. Casey spoke up, "We want to talk to you about the Shoshanna Adair case Bert. Mind coming to the Station with me?"

"What if I say no?"

"We got a subpoena here just in case."

Bert hesitated, rubbing his son's grave marker. "Okay, I'll go." The two state police officers and Casey guided Bert to their police vehicle.

Red Atkins was waiting for Bert as he was led into the interrogation room. After he was read his Miranda rights, Bert agreed to talk to the chief. "I have nothing to hide," he said. Casey, the DA and the state police were in the next room taking notes while watching through the one way window. Casey had surprised Red by asking to remain behind the window with the other investigators.

"Bert, I'm Red Atkins, Chief of detectives here in Ridgewood. We are here to interview you about the Shoshanna Adair murder."

"You're Casey's boss?" assumed Bert.

"Yes, I am."

Red continued, "Her murder occurred five years ago. I don't know if you remember it." Silence greeted him. "I think you were questioned about the murder." Silence again. "Did you know the girl?"

"I remember she worked in a bar," said Bert.

"So you remember?"

"Yes, a bit."

"Do you know that someone left a bomb on her doorstep that blew her up?"

"I remember reading about it."

Red questioned further, "Do you know how to make a bomb Bert?"

Bert looked the chief in the eye, "What kind of question is that? I'm a tool and die guy."

"Funny you should say that Bert. Your co-workers at Armstrong said that you could fix anything. Be it electronics or machines, you were a wiz. The bomb that killed that girl was pretty sophisticated. Not every shmo could have designed a bomb triggered to go off when the package was picked up."

"I don't know what you are talking about. I didn't make any bomb. Anyone could have made it."

Changing course Red asked about the late witness. "Did you know a Linda Halloran Bert? She worked at the bar with Shoshanna. She claims you were obsessed with Shoshanna. Linda reported that Shoshanna was terrified of you."

Bert, getting more agitated responded, "You nuts? I never heard of that girl. I think you have a nut job for a witness."

"Funny you should say that Bert. Linda recently died. Know anything about her death?" Silence and long stares followed between the two men.

Getting tired of this cat and mouse game Red decided to turn the screws tighter on the little man. "So, if we went to your home we would not find any bomb making material?"

For the first time Bert glowered, "You stay out of my home!"

"Why?" asked Red calmly. "Got something to hide Bert?"

Bert pounded the table. "I'm warning you, stay out of my house!"

Red in turn pounded the table. "Enough of this bullshit Bert! We got your DNA from the bomb. It seems some of your cells remained on the stamps you put on the package. Good luck trying to find the billionth person on the planet who shares your exact DNA."

Red watched as the penetrating eyes of Bert seemed to pop out of their sockets. Red could almost read Bert's inner dialogue. The bombing evidence would lead to a search of his home.

Red smiled, "My men are already on their way to your home with a search warrant. Are they going to find anyone there Bert?"

Bert immediately picked up on the "anyone" comment. "I want a lawyer," he demanded.

Chapter 15: Bert's Secrets

CASEY AND KIM WALKED CAUTIOUSLY down the stairs to Bert's basement. "Careful Kim, he could have some wired things down here," said Casey. The basement had an odd, pungent smell – mustiness combined with a chemical odor. A stretcher, covered with a sheet sat in the middle of the basement. Kim gingerly removed the sheet. To her horror, she was face to face with a corpse that had a ghoulish quality. Mostly paper thin skin covered the features of what looked like a woman. The see-through skin revealed cheek and jaw bones. The person was wearing gold earrings, and what looked like red rouge was smeared onto the cheeks.

Kim slowly pulled off the rest of the sheet. The corpse wore a long, blue dress, adorned with white pearls, fit for a wedding. There was a wedding ring on her left hand. Both hands were clasping a bouquet of dried red roses. So fragile was the skin that Kim was afraid to touch the woman for fear a limb would fall off. Kim and Casey then canvassed the rest of the house, but found no other decedents.

The detectives then called Red at the Station, updating him on the situation. "No other bodies there, huh," said an obviously disappointed Red. "Well, call the Medical Examiner's Office. We got to find out who this person is."

Casey was more encouraging, "Maybe it's the woman veteran missing from the Mausoleum, boss."

Kim asked, "What's going on with our suspect?"

"Silent as a rock, just sitting in his cell. He wants an attorney. We got a lot of work to do to get some answers here. Make sure you get his computer and hard drive, and anything else that will help us."

"Will do boss."

Indeed in the next month Ridgewood and State police investigators had their hands full finding out the identity of the basement corpse. Medical examiners soon confirmed that it was a woman of approximately thirty years of age.

This ruled out the woman veteran missing from the Mausoleum, who had died at the age of eighty. Regardless, Red had DNA done on the corpse, which confirmed she was not the veteran from the Mausoleum, simply by age.

The identity however, did fit that of Bert Stoop's wife Abigail, the spouse that Bert declared had abandoned him after their son's death. This led investigators in a whole new direction. But Red was still convinced that someone who kept the corpse of his wife at home had something to do with the Mausoleum case.

Meanwhile, Bert sat stoically in jail, aiming to fight the legal system. He refused to speak to his first public defender, a woman. "I don't want a fucking woman as my lawyer." His second attorney, a male, did not fare much better. In his only court appearance, Bert said that he wanted to act as his own attorney. He also pled not guilty. The Judge took his request under advisement.

Red and his team searched vigorously for any information about Abigail Stoop. Married to Bert in 1994, the former Abigail Davis was twenty-six at the time. The couple's only child, Benjamin, died of SIDS in June, 1998. Three months later Abigail disappeared, and Bert filed a missing person report with the Ridgewood Police.

Abigail was never found. Red reviewed Bert's 1998 statement in which he said that his wife was depressed, and he believed that she likely returned to her family in California. Her only family was a sister Julie Davis, who had merely a distant relationship with her sister. Julie said that the sisters were army brats, who had lived around the world and had attended eight different schools in their youth. Both parents were deceased. Julie had not seen or heard from Abigail for some time, and could not even tell how Abigail landed in Ridgewood. Julie had never met her sister's husband Bert.

"Sad," said Red to himself after reading the file. He fingered a photo of the young mother. In the photo a radiant Abigail held her son lovingly in her arms. Other photos of Abigail seemed almost somber. "A sadness seems to envelope this woman," thought Red. "It looks like the one joy in her life was her son, and she had to bury him at such a young age." Red was able to get dental records from a Ridgewood dentist Abigail had once visited. They confirmed that the deceased was Abigail.

Red then obtained a court order to exhume the Stoops' baby Benjamin. Medical examiners confirmed it was the fully formed corpse of a five month old baby. DNA confirmed it was that of Benjamin Stoop. An autopsy revealed another surprise. The baby had not died of SIDS. The baby's tiny hyoid bone in his neck was cracked; a sign that someone had strangled baby Benjamin.

With all of the forensic information completed, Red called a meeting with Bert and his attorney. Since the Judge had not ruled on his motion, Bert's attorney had to be present. It didn't matter. Bert was in full control. By this point, Bert had pretty much figured out what investigators now knew.

"We know that your wife was in your basement Bert," said Red. "We also know that you killed Shoshanna Adair. How did your son die, Bert? Why don't you just come clean, Bert. Tell us what you did to these women. To your son."

Bert's attorney was about to caution him not to answer. But Bert put his hand up to silence him. "Shut up," said Bert. In control Bert proposed a deal, "I'll talk on two conditions: Number one, take the death penalty off the table; number two, I'll confess. But only to one person – Casey Conley."

Chapter 16: The Confession

Two days later, suspect Bert Stoop and Detective Casey Conley sat across from one another. Still defiant, Bert had picked the time of the interview and how he wanted his coffee prepared. As he sat down he waved to the other interrogators, including Red, watching through the one way mirror from the adjoining room. As for Casey, he had been prepared for the interview by the State Police and Red. He was coached to be forceful and aggressive with a suspect like Bert. Casey felt surprisingly calm, and immersed himself in the evidence as the day of the interview commenced. Red's last words to Casey were, "Get him to reveal where the other nine bodies are."

Bert sat relaxed with his thick arms crossed over his chest, as Casey reiterated the terms of the plea deal, "In exchange for telling us the truth about all your crimes, the State will take the death penalty off the table. Do you understand this Bert?"

"Definitely," said Bert, aggressively leaning forward with those hawkish eyes. His body language saying, "I'm in charge here."

Casey continued, "Let's start with your wife Abigail and son Benjamin, Bert. What happened to them?"

"Well after my son Benjamin died of SIDS, my wife...."

Casey immediately interrupted, "Bert, your son did not die of SIDS. You killed him. We had his body exhumed and examined by a medical examiner. The little hyoid bone in his neck was crushed. You strangled him. I'm going to tell you this only one more time. Give us the full truth or the deal is off."

It was as if the last bit of human decency Bert possessed left him. He did not care if he was defined as a baby killer. "I did what I had to do to make things good for me." By the end of the interview it was as if he was a wild boar, devoid of any compassion.

"Look," Bert said. "I rescued Abigail. When I met her she was a prostitute. She worked along with other girls from state to state. She was passing through Ridgewood when I met her. She needed me to save her. When I saw those eyes, I knew she was the one for me. So I paid the madam $2,000 for her. You see, no one else wanted her. I was the one who saved her. She did everything I wanted – and I mean everything."

Bert watched Casey's reaction with a sneer. Ignoring Bert's desire to probe this issue, Casey offered, "So what happened?"

"At first everything was perfect. I bought Abigail whatever she needed and taught her to cook the foods I like. But after a while she said she wanted to get a job. I didn't want that. I wanted her home with me. She had everything she needed there. Then she said she wanted to have a kid. I didn't want that either. But the more she asked for one I warmed up to the idea. She would stop complaining about a job, so I agreed to a kid."

"So what changed after Benjamin's birth?"

Angrily Bert said, "She did. She became a fucking nut. Benjamin this and Benjamin that. All her energy for him. When I got home from work, all the baby did was cry and shit. I decided I could not live like that. I wanted things back to when I first got Abigail."

"So you killed the baby?" asked a repulsed Casey.

"Yes, that's right. I strangled the kid. It only took a minute. I read up on this SIDS thing and realized how easy it is for kids to die this way."

"How did Abigail react?" asked Casey.

"She just wasn't right. She mumbled about expecting bad things to happen to her. For a time she wouldn't get out of bed, but I got her walking. I took her out a few times to fancy restaurants and she seemed better. Then she started talking about having another baby. That was not going to happen."

"So how did she die?"

"One night, a few months later she must have had a bad dream. She taps me on the shoulder and says, "I know you did it." Half asleep I told her to go back to sleep. But she was never the same. She grew distant. She was always crying. She wouldn't come near me unless it was by force. When she told me she was going to leave me, I realized what I had to do."

"So you strangled her too?"

"Damn right," Bert said with pathetic pride. "Just like with my son. I drugged her first. She didn't suffer."

"So why did you keep her in the house?" asked Casey.

Bert responded as if Casey was the crazy one for asking the question, "She was mine. I saved her. I was happy with her until the kid came along. Keeping her made all the sense in the world."

Casey choked a bit asking the next question. "Did you have sex with her corpse?"

"A man has needs. I have not done that in years. I read about human preservation and injected her with formaldehyde every few weeks. Don't you think she looked great?" Bert snickered.

By now, sitting in this small office with this diminutive, perverse man, Casey felt like he was in a Twilight Zone universe. Normalcy was foreign in this world. "Tell me about the Shoshanna Adair murder."

"What's to tell? The girl reminded me of my wife. A lost kid with a sad smile. Always jabbering about her kid."

"So how did you meet her?"

"I went into her bar a couple of times after work, and struck up a conversation. She looked like the type of girl who wanted to be rescued."

"She didn't want you to rescue her Bert."

"She led me on. She said we might go to coffee one day, then she changed her mind. I went out of my way to tell her I could help her get her kid back from the State. I read up on the State's child protective services rules, and I talked to her about that at the bar."

Looking down at his hands, Bert started rubbing them forcibly. "At first she was interested in me. Then one night when I was waiting for her after work to talk more, she pulled a nutty. She threatened to call the cops on me. Imagine, a loser like that trying to hurt me when I was trying to help her. So I made the bomb."

"How did you make the bomb Bert?"

Bert seemed to have a sense of pride in his work. "I read up on it. All the parts I could, I got at Armstrong. The hard part was the triggering of the bomb. It detonated when she took the ribbon off the package and opened the lid." He laughed, "I read that many of the bombers blow themselves up making that part."

"Where were you when the bomb went off Bert?"

"I hid and watched it. My biggest fear was that someone else in the building would open it. But I saw her come out. It worked like a charm."

Casey could not help himself. "You must have been real proud," he said cynically. How about Linda Halloran?"

Bert smiled. He seemed to again weigh telling the truth. "She was half-dead anyway. It cost only $200 to have someone give her the hot eight-ball. (Casey knew in drug lingo the eight ball was a

134

combination of heroin with strong opiates.) I wouldn't have even known about the case if you hadn't said something Casey. I knew then I had to shut the kid up."

In the observation room Red and Kim were surprised by this news. "So you knew Linda Halloran?" Casey almost whispered, his face red and sweating.

"Sure, she and Shoshanna were always behind the bar together. I figured Shoshanna told Linda about me. He glared at Casey with a smirk. "If Linda hadn't left town I would have killed her years ago."

"Anything else you want to say Bert? Any other crimes to confess," croaked Casey.

"Yes," said Bert, with a smirk on his face. "Since you are such a good detective kid, I'm going to help you solve another murder. The guy Al Springer is buried behind the nursery at the cemetery. I heard he was mouthing off that I killed my wife. I had to shut him up. I put a bullet in his head on morning when he left the Mausoleum. He should have kept his mouth shut."

After digesting the news of another murder by this serial killer, Casey sprung the trap he and Red had rehearsed. "What about the nine bodies missing from the Mausoleum?" "Where are they?" Casey asked softly.

Bert responded immediately, like a tiger hunting his prey. "You're not the only one who's been looking in basements Casey. Yes, I saw you peering into my basement. I had to control myself not to wave to you. I hope you enjoyed what you saw. I know you did. But you weren't the only one snooping around looking in windows. Yes, I saw you with your nine friends. You are just like me Casey. That's why I wanted you here today. I knew from the first time I saw you in the cemetery that we were alike. The only thing I figured wrong was that you would keep this our little secret. Now, why don't you tell your friends in the window where the bodies are."

As if shot by Bert's words, Casey staggered out of the chair. He put his hands to his head as Bert laughed derisively. "You're just like me Casey," reverberated in the detective's head.

The other detectives in the adjoining room were not making sense of this dynamic. They ran into the room to attend to Casey. It was no use, however. Casey ran through their arms. Red remembered later that Casey let out a sound like a wounded animal. Cops pursued Casey as he raced away in his vehicle.

Meanwhile Bert just sat back and smiled in full satisfaction. His hands resting on his stomach, all he needed was a toothpick to savor this tragic human feast.

Chapter 17: Red's Conflict

RED ATKINS REACHED DOWN and patted Apache, who sat comfortably under his desk. It was the only thing that seemed to give him any pleasure these days. Each day they went for a walk together. The only place Red would not take his new friend was Ridgewood Cemetery. The place was too familiar and Red hoped to never set foot in it again.

It was January 2012, a new year and hopefully a better one than the last. But Red did not really think so. "A black cloud is over me. I need a change," he thought. Indeed in front of him were his retirement papers from the Ridgewood Police Department. He had not signed them yet. They had sat staring at him for the last week.

"I'm sure the Mayor won't object now," considered Red. It had been a bad couple of months for his Department. Red saw town workers and residents give him a sideways glance and put their heads together whispering things. "How could one of their own, a police detective, be responsible for taking nine bodies out of the Mausoleum?" "How could they not find the bodies for almost a year, when the perpetrator was so close?"

The last weeks were like a blur to Red. The nine missing decedents, eight men and one woman, were found in Casey Conley's basement mudroom; in the house donated to the decorated amputee veteran by the good citizens of Ridgewood. Casey's body, killed by a self-inflicted gunshot from his police revolver, was also found there. Casey beat the Ridgewood police department to his home by ten minutes. That was enough time to put a gun to his temple. When the officers entered they saw Casey, lying in the center of the room, surrounded by the nine bodies that rested on stretchers. Apache, nestled beside Casey, nudged him from time to time, trying to awaken him.

Medical Examiners studied all of the Mausoleum victims. They were all in remarkably good shape. The basement of the home was cool and dry – perfect conditions for the embalmed bodies. The Medical Examiners all agreed on one thing: the deceased had not been mutilated or disrupted in any way. They were all fully clothed and each had an American flag tucked under their hands.

Red had arranged for all nine victims to be recommitted to their crypts in the Mausoleum. The families were present as rabbis, pastors, and priests rededicated the spots from which their loved ones would never be moved again. Military Honor guards escorted the decedents while the sounds of trumpets playing TAPS reverberated nine times through the marble walls. The families multiple lawsuits also continued their way through the criminal legal system. The Ridgewood Police Department, and the estate of Casey Conley were now defendants.

Red attended all the services, and apologized to all the families, despite the admonitions of city attorneys. He felt responsible in multiple ways. He had recruited Casey to his detective squad. More importantly, he loved Casey, and berated himself because he had failed to help him. Red failed to perceive Casey's strange affect and attitude toward the Mausoleum case. He failed to notice that Casey declined to discuss his personal life and demons. He failed to press Casey, a fellow veteran obviously in the throes of FTSD, to get therapy. Red had failed his friend Casey because he had missed all these signs.

Red arranged for Casey's sparsely attended funeral. Present were Casey's parents, some colleagues, and a young woman Red had never met. She introduced herself to Red as Lily. Red insisted on an Honor Guard for Casey's funeral, although the veterans' officer initially objected. The young lady dabbed her eyes during the tribute, then quietly and quickly left the cemetery.

Red's failures were physically obvious. "Red" no longer applied. The remaining red remnants of his hair turned white in a month. He lost ten pounds, and lines that never existed before, appeared on his face. His hands now trembled when he picked up a file to read.

Part of his agitation related to the burial of Abigail Stoop and her son Benjamin. Red had arranged for both of them to be buried together in one casket, never to be separated again. He paid for the funeral and bought the grave. But there was a hitch. Their killer, Bert Stoop, was still the next of kin. Bert had to approve the funeral arrangements that Red had coordinated. Not surprisingly, Bert who was tucked away in Ridgewood State Prison ninety miles away for the rest of his life, wanted to be present. Red had to agree.

So on the day of the service a priest blessed the bodies of Abigail and her son as the casket was lowered into the grave. Bert, in his orange jumpsuit, his hands in handcuffs and his legs in chains, watched in silence. He had a large smirk on his face, acting like the conductor of the orchestra turning to face his captivated audience. "I suppose you found Springer's body exactly where I told you."

Red could not be denied, "You're a real prick Bert. I hope you rot in hell." In fact, Red had found Al's body buried near the nursery just as Bert had said. A bullet in Al's head matched Bert's gun, which had been confiscated. It was yet another burial Red had to help coordinate with Al's widow.

Red's comment seemed to enliven Bert, as he returned to the correction vehicle with his two guards. Red was later helped to understand that for people like Bert, sociopaths, any recreation of their crime was like heroin to a junkie. It made his wretched body come alive.

So Red sat gloomily at his desk on this cold January day, contemplating his future. He then got a surprising phone call. It was from Winnifred "Winnie" Albert, the retired FBI profiler whom he had hired to help him with the Mausoleum investigation.

"How are you, Red? I've been following the case. I'm so sorry it was resolved this way."

"Thank you Winnie. Yes, it's been very difficult for me. I wish I could have helped Casey. Obviously, his actions had something to do with his war experience. I know he had lost two very close friends over there."

"How about I come up there and reexamine the case. Part of what I do as a profiler is to understand the perpetrators' motives. Like how did their inner world fit with the crime? Or what psychological forces motivated them?"

"That would be great Winnie, but I can't afford that, responded Red. "The Mayor is still on me about your fees for the initial work."

"This one's a freebie Red. This is my passion. I don't just do it for the money. If my data helps solve even one future crime, I'm satisfied."

"Well, great then. Come on up."

"Oh, there's one condition," said Winnie. "I want complete access to your files, including Bert Stoop. I want to understand the origins of his pathology."

"No problem. When can you be here?"

"Tomorrow."

To Red, this was the best news he had heard in months.

Chapter 18: "You weren't just like me"

THE NEXT DAY AT EXACTLY 11:00 AM, Winnifred "Winnie" Albert walked into the dilapidated Ridgewood Police Station. With all due respect to his detective Kim, Red thought to himself, "Winnie pretties up this poor place." The retired behavioral analyst for the FBI was fashionably attired, with tailored slacks and a red sweater. Her long black hair was curled to frame her face. She carried herself with professional poise, and immediately went to work.

Sitting at Casey's old desk for several days, Winnie studied every nuance of the files on Bert and Casey. She examined the photographs and forensic material regarding the murders of Abigail and Benjamin Stoop, and Linda Halloran, as well as the crime scene at Casey's home. She ate her lunch, always a ham and cheese on rye, at her desk, affording her more time to examine the case.

On the fourth day, Red prevailed upon Winnie to allow him to take her to lunch. "This is the least

I can do for you, Winnie. I can't thank you enough for giving your time to this case."

Over another ham and cheese at the deli, Winnie revealed that her son was a freshman at college. "Red, I have all the time in the world now. This is not work for me. Working as a behavioral profiler is who I am."

The lunch extended two hours. Red learned that Winnie and her husband, a former FBI agent had divorced three years ago. "Our son probably kept us together longer than we should have," is all she said.

Red was so comfortable in the long lunch that he divulged some of his own personal life. He discussed his brief marriage and his painful estrangement from his two children. He disclosed his ambivalence about his retirement.

Eventually, their discussion centered on Winnie's career. "How did you get into this line of work?" asked Red. Winnie hesitated, a brief pause in her professional poise. "I grew up in an abusive home. My father was a bank president, and an alcoholic. He was also abusive to my mother. As the oldest, with a younger sister, I learned early how to protect the members of my family. I studied what topics made my dad upset, and learned how to calm him down.

When I saw him getting angry, I would jump in his lap, and tell him he was the greatest and kindest dad in the world. I guess this started my curiosity about human motivation."

Red was inquisitive, "So when you examine a case, what are you looking for?

"In general Red, I am looking beyond the motive. I am looking at the gratification that these crimes provided to Casey and Bert. The crime itself tells us a lot about the suspect: Was the crime organized, and well-planned out? Certainly our Mausoleum case here required careful planning in order to be this successful, right Red? Same with Bert's pride in his bomb. Or was it a random, impulsive act? Was the victim simply in the wrong place at the wrong time? This leads to a chaotic crime scene. That is certainly not the situation here."

Winnie continued, "I also look into the suspect's background. Does this person have military training? Is the person well educated? What might his family of origin look like? From a portrait of similar criminals I can often predict personality patterns, and what motivated them."

"So where is your investigation going now?" asked Red.

"Now that I've examined the paperwork, I will be out of the office for a few days. I want to interview anyone who will talk to me, including Bert Stoop. I want to interview Casey's family and some of his army colleagues. I want to interview his old girlfriend Lily."

"I see," said Red, now aware that her investigation could take some time. He was also aware that Winnie lived two hundred miles from Ridgewood, and she was staying at a local Holiday Inn. "Look, I can't pay for your hotel, but

I have a proposal. I live in a big house all alone here in Ridgewood, just me and Apache. If you like you could stay in my house while you complete your work. Obviously, I am a gentleman."

Winnie smiled, "The FBI pension is not great. Maybe I'll take you up on that offer."

So over the next few days Winnie stayed at Red's house, as she conducted her behavioral interviews. He didn't see her much, but made a point to have dinner ready for her every night. He even bought flowers for his dining room table. Their discussions became more and more personal, to the point that it was hard to deny their attraction to one another. One night Red finally made known his feelings, "I feel like a high school kid around you Winnie. I would like to get to know you better, but I'm not sure if you feel the same way. It's been a long time since I've had these feelings."

Winnie hesitated a bit before answering. "Red, for a person like me relationships are difficult. My profile work is so intense I often forget to examine my needs as much as I should. I have spent so much time trying to understand why I married a controlling husband, and as importantly why I stayed so long in that relationship. I love my freedom, and will not compromise on that issue." Then smiling she added, "But I must admit Red that you are the nicest guy I have met since my divorce. How about if we take things slow, and see how our relationship evolves?"

"I totally understand," said Red. "I'll take this relationship, if that's what it is, as slow as you need. All I can say is I love your independent nature. It's what first attracted me to you."

A month later, Winnie was done with her interviews, but remained at Red's home. After dinner and wine one evening, Red hesitantly leaned over to kiss Winnie. Winnie surprised herself with the ardor of her response. Things escalated from there, their awkwardness with one another dissipating quickly. Each unleased a passion in one another that had been repressed for a long time.

One night, as they lay in each other's arms, Red started to cry. He had not cried since he left Vietnam. "I should have been able to help Casey," he confessed. "Why did he take those bodies?" And it was there, in Red's arms that Winnie softly stated, "You could not have helped Casey, Red."

The next morning Red, happier than he'd been for a long time, arose to the aromas of coffee and bacon coming from the kitchen. As Red and Winnie sat down to breakfast, Red asked Winnie if she really believed he couldn't have helped Casey. Winnie shared with him her professional findings. "You could not have helped Casey, Red. His crime was a coalition of a dysfunctional youth with the physical and emotional trauma of the war. You see Casey felt dead inside, and the only comfort came from surrounding himself with the dead. He developed a fantasy life, and in that life the dead veterans were the only ones he could trust. Their presence allowed Casey to feel that the men who gave their lives for him, Zaggy, and Quinny, were still alive."

"You see Red, Casey came from a family that damaged his self-esteem. His mother was controlling and demanding. He was afraid to share his feelings with her. This breeds resentment and anger in a young boy, and for a sensitive boy like Casey, tremendous guilt for hating his mother. This never ending cycle of anger and guilt gets buried, but not eliminated. This was combined with an alcoholic father, who provided little in the way of a male role model. Casey then grew up feeling weird and different from anyone else, even though all youths experience this in varying degrees. In his case, Casey had no one to trust, no one to share his insecurities with. Again, it's a self-defeating and repetitive identity problem that was never resolved. Maybe if he had had a healthy mentor, like an uncle perhaps, who could have normalized his thoughts, he might have had a better self-identity."

"There was one small way Casey was like Bert, Red. With his self-esteem so damaged, Casey's psyche scrambled to control something – anything. In adolescence he focused first on his career, and then on Lily. This gave him some semblance of peace of mind, especially knowing he had Lily. She gave him a confidence he had never experienced, to share his feelings with someone. But having had no role models, Casey's view of intimacy was different than yours and mine. To him, love was like a treasured possession – something to adore, perfect in every way, but also fragile. It could not sustain any mistakes, betrayals, or imperfections. I can see Casey surrounded by those nine decedents. He was aware that he could not be hurt or disappointed by them, as he had by the living."

Winnie continued, "Lily told me that Casey was not sure he wanted children. Again, a feeling shared with Bert. But their reasons were different. Bert cared only about himself, and his needs. He could command his wife to fulfill those needs until she turned her focus on her child. Casey seemed to have a fantasy like image of intimacy in that there was only so much love to go around. He committed all his love to Lily. There would be nothing left for a child. And in his mind Lily would not have enough love for him if there was a child. His struggle with intimacy emanated from a loveless home, so in a way he created a love out of his own poor experiences."

Red offered, "Do you think if Casey had not gone to war the couple would have lasted?'

Winnie hesitated, and then said, "Not sure, but I doubt it. Again, cracks were appearing in the relationship even before the war. Casey learned to hide portions of himself, even from Lily. When I interviewed Lily, she told me that Casey was very possessive of her. She began to see his desperation in a dependence that disturbed her. 'He loved me so much, it scared me sometimes Winnie,' were Lily's exact words. She told me that she never knew what Casey was really thinking." Winnie sighed, "Little did Lily know that Casey was a mystery even to himself."

Winnie gazed thoughtfully, "The big question for me Red, is why didn't Casey seek out therapy when he lost his leg, and his friends. This was his last chance to heal. My guess is that by that time Casey was a hopeless loser in his own mind. His self-esteem was so damaged he could not see a way out. He could not trust anyone."

"But why did he commit suicide, Winnie?" asked a puzzled Red.

"Well, Casey panicked when you solved the common denominator in the victims, Red, their veteran status. He knew that a good detective like you would solve the case, and he saw you closing in on him. Casey now had a decision to make. He could be selfish, and pin the crime on Bert. He analyzed that, even though Bert could never produce the decedents. The suspicions could eliminate Casey as a suspect. Or, he could endure the public humiliation of admitting to his crime. The public would see just how sick Casey felt about himself."

For a sensitive and basically good person like Casey, this was a pivotal decision. His helplessness turned to hopelessness, and he made the decision to blame someone else for his crime. He hated himself, even if that someone was a sociopath like Bert Stoop. When Bert confronted Casey with his own secret, the guilt was too much for him. Bert knew just what to say to tighten Casey's anguish; his words cut like a knife.. 'You're just like me.' "

Winnie continued, "As for Bert, my biggest decision was whether he was a psychopath or a sociopath. Bert had a sociopathic personality. Psychopaths, Red, have a disruption in their brain activity. They simply do not register sympathy and guilt in their neurons. In fact as you probably know, some guilty people routinely pass a lie detector test. That is the psychopath. Their neurons do not have a path to the guilt regions of the brain. Sociopaths, however, choose to ignore any guilt or the feelings of others. They are consumed with manipulation and control – anything to satisfy their own needs. So they are narcissists, which is a common diagnosis today. But for serial killers like Bert, they are narcissists with a powerful rage. They have a unique ability to "hoard" rage. They also consider themselves special, and any loss of control or rejection is fatal for those around them."

Red was listening intently, and asked, "Why is that?"

"Because buried deep in their subconscious, these manipulative people have intense feelings of inadequacy. Their over reactive rage salvages their fragile egos – how could they do that to me? Sociopaths feel they, themselves are the ultimate victims. So in Bert's mind, his victims got what they deserve."

"When I examined Bert's family history, he did not come from one of abuse or neglect. In fact, Bert's sister told me the he was their parents' favored child. He could do no wrong. His antisocial behavior started early, however. He had many fights with classmates, and once threatened to burn his teacher's house down. He had few friends, and the one he had was arrested with Bert for starting a fire in the school restroom. Impulsive behavior like this is common. Bert easily justified his behavior, because people were simply objects around him to be used. When Bert hurts someone he is unleashing a lifetime of pocketed rage that someone has to pay for. That explains why Bert had to see Shoshanna blow up."

Red and Winnie moved over to the couch, and Winnie nestled in Red's arms. "So let's take the murders one at a time. Bert killed his wife because he felt he owned her. I've never worked on such a blatant case where the criminal wore his need for power and control on his sleeve. In fact, most sociopaths learn to be charming, disguising their callousness even while considering others worthless. Not Bert. He paid for Abigail and she was his. Her desire to leave him, her rejection, meant his loss of control. He could not have that."

"So his keeping her was not about sex?" asked Red.

"Necrophilia is not well understood, Red, even by researchers. But what is known is that it is less about sex, and more about domination. Bert's "thrill" was having total power over someone even in death. His baby, Benjamin, simple expediency. He did not want this "kid." Again, the baby was an object to a person like Bert. He had the ability to control life and death over someone, and he made his choice."

Red then asked about Shoshanna Adair. Winnie sighed, "I wish I had more data about this poor girl, Red. For some reason this girl triggered some fantasy in Bert's mind that drew him to her. She probably reminded him of Abigail. Her rejection of him, after he drew her into his dangerous orbit, resulted in his feelings of rage. Rage so seething that he methodically built a bomb and planned her assassination. With all the effort this took he could not miss the event. He watched from his vehicle while Shoshanna was blown to bits."

Red was shaking his head in disbelief, "He told you this?"

"Yes, he said he even took a picture of the remnants of the bombing. In our business, we call these "trophies". The criminals rehash the crime with objects, clothing, or jewelry that were owned by their victims. This renews their initial gratification. It is similar to a sexual experience – indeed many criminals masturbate after touching these "trophies."

Red felt dirty even listening to Winnie's explanations, dirty that he was part of a human group that included Bert. He then asked Winnie about Linda Halloran.

"Again, simple expediency. She was going to hurt Bert, so she had to go. Unfortunately, to a person like Bert it was as simple as tying one's shoes. This also contributed to Casey's self-abuse. Bert reminded Casey that his investigation led to Linda's death, don't forget. That was probably the last straw that drew Casey to kill himself. This logic applies to Al Springer also. He was an object to Bert. You see how easy killing now came to Bert – a true serial killer. He killed two people within a month, as simple as brushing his teeth. And he would have kept on killing, even you Red."

"So tell me about your interview with Bert," said Red.

"Well, I'm surprised he even agreed to see me," said Winnie. "Women in particular are like objects to him. He certainly emanates evil. He didn't even pretend to show a good side of himself." Winne's mind took her back to the interview with Bert...

Winnie's first thoughts when she came face to face with Bert were that his physical stature, his skin now prison white, emphasized his soulless black eyes. He laughed about Casey, saying, "Imagine that guy trying to pin those bodies on me! He deserved what he got."

The rest of the brief interview had Bert bragging about his crimes. He said none would have died if they did not try to hurt him. Winnie asked, "Even Benjamin?" Bert's face had no emotion as he answered, "That was Abigail's fault. I didn't want it."

Ignoring the "it" comment, Winnie asked about Shoshanna's bombing. "I was proud of that one," bragged Bert. "It worked like a charm."

"Is that why you wanted to watch her get blown up?"

"Damn right. As a matter of fact, I used to read all the newspaper accounts of the bombing over and over." Bert laughed, "Isn't that what you people call a trophy? Yes, I enjoyed reading about it." Then suddenly turning to the prison guards,

Bert yelled, "Now get me the fuck out of here. I'm done with her."

Winnie just stared as Bert sneered at her....

Looking intently into Red's eyes, Winnie said, "So you see Red, Casey and Bert could not be more different. Casey was a good man consumed with guilt and shame. I would call him what is known as a romantic necrophilia. He needed these people around him to relieve him of his dead feelings inside. Those veterans' bodies symbolized his friends – Zaggy and Quinny – who sacrificed their lives for someone who did not deserve rescuing. There were probably some unconscious impulses within Casey related to life and death. He achieved a bit of mental comfort having those bodies with him. He defeated death, and he could protect his deceased military colleagues."

"As for Bert, he chose to view his victims as objects. In my work with serial killers like Bert, I compare them to lions prowling the savanna for food. They have a need – hunger – that must be fulfilled. There is no room for compassion or guilt in this narcissistic pursuit. In Bert's case that hunger was more perverse. The act itself – the thrill of complete power to end someone's life – was the only way to satiate this hunger."

Red stood up, "I'm sorry Winnie. I don't feel well. She next heard him vomit in the bathroom.

Chapter 19: Epilogue

RED WHEELED THE NEW FORTY-FOOT MOTOR HOME into his driveway. It had a main bedroom, luxury kitchen, and even a fireplace. Winnie, a travel pack on her lap said, "I think the first park we see is Yellowstone." The married couple was embarking on a three month odyssey to see as many of the sixty-three National Parks as possible. As Winnie spoke, their dog Apache sat comfortably at Winnie's feet, a mild reminder of the couple's introduction to one another three years earlier.

Lots of things have happened in those three years. When Red invited Winnie to stay with him as she investigated both Casey and Bert, neither she nor Red could have predicted that she would never leave. In fact, the only exception was when she left to sell her own home. Six months after meeting Winnie, Red put in his retirement papers. At Winnie's urging, Red reached out more aggressively to spend time with his son and daughter. To his surprise, the more mature, post college children were amenable to seeing him. Red's best Christmas had occurred last year when his son and daughter joined Winnie and her son Owen to celebrate the holiday at his home. It was the first time the Christmas presents he sent every year to his children were not returned. He relished in the joy he saw on his children's faces when they opened their gifts. As time went on, Winnie's son, a medical student in Boston, also developed a close relationship with Red's children.

In the past two years the couple had made it a mission to educate veterans about the crippling effects of untreated PTSD. They toured across the country in their Winnebago, and each shared their specific knowledge of the condition at various meetings and gatherings. They used Casey as an example to show how the love he had for his fellow veterans could become so twisted. Many veterans later came up to the couple to thank them for normalizing what they considered their own "crazy" thoughts. Even the families of the nine veterans stolen from the Mausoleum came to forgive Casey. They realized the war hero was a damaged soul, who in his own way actually cared for their loved ones.

A year ago the happy couple, now age sixty, spontaneously decided to get married. It was a validation of their love, an emotion neither had felt for many years.

Casey's father died a year after Casey. Dan had stopped going to his watering hole at the "V" despite the entreaties of his bar mates. He even stopped drinking in tribute to his "hero" son. His damaged kidneys failed him soon after his recovery, however.

A year after her husband died, Casey's mom remarried. She married one of her late husband's drinking buddies from the "V". Neighbors of the couple often hear Casey's mom yelling at her new husband, "I don't know why I have to clean up after a loser like you."

Lily took Casey's death badly, and for a long time blamed herself. She finally embarked on a relationship with a life coach, which changed her life. Lily married two years later, and was now expecting her first child. She fulfilled her dream to be a teacher. Second graders in a nearby town were greeted by her smiling face each school day.

As for Bert Stoop, he sat in protective custody in the State Prison for twenty-three hours per day. He often declines to leave his cell for the one hour he is allowed outside. Prison guards have a sinister nickname for him: "the Toad."

Prison officials had to remove Bert from the general population for his own protection. He often bragged about the bomb he built to "blow up my girlfriend." His narcissism grated on fellow inmates in other ways. The other prisoners often referred to him as "Vampire" given his relationship with his dead wife. Ever the narcissist, Bert would quip, "My dead wife was better than your living wife." It is reported that the lifers were fighting over who would put a shiv in Bert. Hence his isolation in protective custody.

A simple grave marker sits in Ridgewood Cemetery. It reads: Casey Parker Conley, 1982-

2011. His quiet grave has a frequent visitor, Jim Boyd, the cemetery's longest tenured employee. Jim frequently adorns the simple stone with angels and cherubs that he rubs from nearby graves. He often speaks quietly to Casey, nodding his head as he says, "I know why you took them Casey. You loved them." Perhaps Jim, the caretaker, understood the complex Casey best.

ABOUT THE AUTHOR

Stephen Rocco is a third-generation funeral director in a funeral home outside of Boston. In addition to working as a funeral director over 40 years, he was a family mediator. He was an instructor at Mt Ida College for many years and Co-Director of its National Center For Death Education. Stephen and his wife, Lidia, have been blessed with four children and three grandchildren (and hopefully many more).